MIRROR OF TRANSFORMATIONS

To Fiona
with kindest regards.
Rita Way

Rita Lawrance
March '0d

Rita Lawrance was born in Hammersmith in 1928. At the age of 11 she was sent away with her brother John as an evacuee during World War II. After the war she did secretarial work of different kinds, moving from one unsatisfying job to another until she became a clinical secretary in cancer research – job satisfaction at last. When she moved to Middlesex with her husband, Basil, she worked for two hospitals and a GP before becoming a full-time housewife. She has become a compulsive writer of short stories. There are more in the pipeline – so watch this space.

MIRROR OF TRANSFORMATIONS

Rita Lawrance

MIRROR OF TRANSFORMATIONS

Olympia Publishers
London

www.olympiapublishers.com
OLYMPIA PAPERBACK EDITION

Copyright © Rita Lawrance 2009

The right of Rita Lawrance to be identified as author of
this work has been asserted in accordance with sections 77 and 78 of
the Copyright, Designs and Patents Act 1988.

All Rights Reserved

No reproduction, copy or transmission of this publication
may be made without written permission.
No paragraph of this publication may be reproduced,
copied or transmitted save with the written permission of the
publisher, or in accordance with the provisions
of the Copyright Act 1956 (as amended).

Any person who does any unauthorized act in relation to
this publication may be liable to criminal
prosecution and civil claims for damage.

A CIP catalogue record for this title is
available from the British Library.

ISBN: 978-1-905513-81-9

This is a work of fiction.
Names, characters, places and incidents originate from the writer's
imagination. Any resemblance to actual persons, living or dead, is
purely coincidental.

First Published in 2009

Olympia Publishers
60 Cannon Street
London
EC4N 6NP

Printed in Great Britain

Dedication

This is for my husband Basil for all the years of support and encouragement. He's a diamond.

Acknowledgement

My thanks to Dr Dominique Collon, formerly of the British Museum, for her help with archaeological details. By an amazing coincidence she too was on an official dig in Iraq 35 years before the story BY THE RIVERS OF BABYLON was written

CONTENTS

By The Rivers Of Babylon 17
Miss Henshaw, Paracelcus and Khubla Khan 30
The Birth Of Danny Doubleday 39
Tunnellers and Grobbledingers 47
Lady Of Secrets 58
Tidal Wave 63
A Pot Of Earl Grey 69
Epona's Well 76
Love Is Blind 85
The Angel and the Spider 90
The Changelings 97
The Bytings 104
Murder Most Fouled-Up 120
A Tree, A Serpent and A Staff 125
Finding Sparkie 132
The Rainbow Came and Went 137
Mirror Of Transformations 143

By The Rivers Of Babylon

Two elderly archeologists sat drinking coffee in a London flat. Professor David Schulberg and Professor Michael O'Leary had not met since they had worked together thirty-five years ago. In those days they used to call each other Mick and Dave, and the old camaraderie had instantly re-emerged when they had met at a railway station an hour before.

"And now," said Mick, whose flat it was, "we had better stop gossiping so that I can tell you why I wanted us to meet again."

After a short silence Dave said, "Yes? I'm listening."

Mick cleared his throat, looking around the room. "Oh hell!" he said at last. "Look, ditch that coffee. Let's have a drop of Irish whisky." He got up with some difficulty and began to set out glasses on the table between them, and then brought a bottle of whisky to the table. For a few minutes they discussed the relative merits of Scotch and Irish liquor.

"OK. So now shall we cut to the chase?" suggested Dave.

Mick took a deep breath. "Alright. Send your mind back to 1972."

Dave's hand tightened around his glass and the fingers of his other hand curled inwards.

"We were with a team," continued Mick, "excavating the ruins of an ancient city on the banks of the River Euphrates in Iraq."

"Haven't you forgotten something?" said Dave quietly.

"What?"

"We vowed never to speak of it again."

Mick looked away. "Just let me continue. We discovered a clay tablet impressed with cuneiform writing. We knew it would end up in Baghdad Museum, so we photographed it and translated the writing in the usual way, then took it to the findings tent with the other trophies. The writing was a message giving the whereabouts of a great treasure hidden in caves 'due west of Babylon'. We knew where the ruins of Babylon were, so we arranged with the Iraqis to go there the following year."

"Yes," said Dave. "I remember the Iraqi official reminding us that anything we might find belonged to their government. Meanwhile, the clay tablet would remain hidden in the museum archives because any passing scholar would be able to translate the message and become… excited, shall we say?"

The two men fell silent, each with his own thoughts – Mick anxious and Dave troubled.

Eventually Mick spoke. "Do you remember the message?"

"Of course."

"Tell me."

"OK. '*I, servant of the Great King…*' "

"Who would have been Cyrus the Second at the level we were digging…"

"Yes – '*I servant of the Great King and last custodian of the Terrible Secret, am about to die. There is no man around me I can trust to keep the Secret. Whosoever finds this message will become the next custodian because Anu, God of Heaven who sees all, will have guided him. Due west of Babylon is a great treasure which we stole from our enemies a generation ago and hid in one of many caves. If discovered, the enemy would sacrifice many lives to recover it. It is a thing of great and terrible power which must never be discovered, unless by wise men who would save the world. Anu will know you and appoint you guardian. You must look at the Terrible Treasure just once. Hereby is recorded exact directions. When you find the Evening Frog you will have found the cave. Take care to veil your face before you look. Seal again the place of concealment and always keep the Secret. May Anu guide your footsteps. Farewell*'."

Mick gave a deep sigh and nodded. "Yes, I too can recite that in my sleep. Now let's look at what happened next. We mounted an expedition of our own the following year…"

***

The Iraqi official spoke perfect English with just the trace of an accent. "Well, gentlemen, I think that covers all the official documents. The main thing to remember is that should you find anything of interest – shall we say – it automatically belongs to my government. You touch nothing. I apologise for having to confiscate your cameras. You have, of course, told nobody else except your last year's team?"

"Nobody," affirmed Dave. "The team has been sworn to secrecy."

The official rose. "Then, gentlemen, I think I need keep you no longer. Omar here is to be your official escort. I should perhaps point out that those caves have been explored for many years and nothing of note has ever been found. They are of interest to geologists, but normally nobody else except tourists. I wish you a safe journey and the best of luck."

***

The search had been fruitless and was nearing its end when their Iraqi escort had an accident. He was hurrying towards the other two men over a rocky outcrop, calling, "There's a small cave up here we missed!" when his foot stumbled on some loose scree, wrenching his left ankle and causing him to fall heavily on a cluster of jagged rocks.

Dave and Mick ran to him. Dave supported him whilst Mick examined him.

"Ankle!" Omar gasped. "Side hurts!"

"Omar, can you try taking a deep breath?"

Omar shook his head. Mick gently pressed the man's side, which made Omar yelp.

"Sorry, old chap, but I think you've got one or two broken ribs there, and I'm afraid your ankle's broken. We'll have to get you into the back of the Land Rover and take you to the nearest hospital."

"Just seen… small cave… we missed…" gasped Omar.

"Doesn't matter, we've missed lots anyway," said Dave. "Don't try to talk. We'll look at your cave when we get back. Right now you need a strong painkiller so that we can settle you comfortably in the back of the old Rover."

***

"Didn't look much to me," said Mick as they emerged from Omar's cave. "Small and insignificant. Let's just sit down over there and rest for a minute."

"Don't let's stay too long. I'm starving and I want to make a meal before nightfall."

They dropped their backpacks and sat on the ground. It was late afternoon and colours were shifting and changing as the sun moved towards the west.

Dave gave a sudden sharp intake of breath, and then whispered, "What in God's name's that?"

"What?"

"Look at that boulder near the cave entrance. It seems to change shape as the sun moves. What does it look like to you right now?"

Mike gazed at the boulder, then gave a shout of excitement. "Yes! A frog! A crouching frog!"

"My friend, if I'm not mistaken it seems we might have found the 'Evening Frog' of the tablet!" said Dave, scarcely able to control his voice.

They looked at each other in amazement, and then scrambled to their feet, put on their backpacks and hurried back towards the cave.

"Small and insignificant? The very place to hide something, wouldn't you say?" said Mick as they reached the entrance. "Here we go then."

They took off their backpacks and found their torches and battery-operated lamps again. The lamps shed an eerie light around the cave as the evening deepened outside.

"Nothing," said Mick.

"We both saw the frog," insisted Dave. "We weren't imagining it. There's got to be something." He shone his torch upwards and peered at the ceiling. "Nothing there, and nothing anywhere else. Tell you what – why don't we leave it and go back and have a meal? We'll feel more like exploring in the morning, and there'll be some daylight from the entrance too."

"I can't believe you're saying that! We actually found the frog, didn't we? So let's go."

"Mick, we're both tired and hungry. When we come back in the morning we shall both be at our best and can give it full attention. Now come on!" Dave turned and walked purposefully away.

As they left the cave, Mick took one regretful glance back and swept the beam of his torch around the little cave. Then something caught his attention.

"Dave!"

Dave stopped picking his way over the loose scree and looked back over his shoulder. "What?"

"Quick – come and look at this!"

Dave drew level to where Mick was shining his torch and peered into the cave. "What are you looking at?"

"Look right at the back."

Dave looked. "I can't see anything out of the ordinary."

Mick stepped aside a few inches. "It doesn't show up from where you're standing. Come closer."

Dave did so but could still see nothing.

"Wait here!"

Mick strode into the cave towards the back and disappeared. "See what I mean?" came his disembodied voice.

"What the hell... where are you, for God's sake!"

"It's an optical illusion! A natural one!" called Mick, reappearing as suddenly as he had vanished. "See? Hey presto!"

Dave ran towards the back and stared at the rock wall. Mick raised his right arm horizontally and it vanished. He laughed at his friend's bewilderment as he brought the arm back again.

"There's a gap here, but from a distance – even from where you're standing – looking like a solid continuous wall. Come closer."

Dave stepped forward and gasped. "You're absolutely right, and yet only a matter of inches away you wouldn't notice." He stepped backwards. "Now I'm about a foot away and it looks like a solid wall. So what's behind it?"

"It looks like a passage of some sort, perhaps only a few feet long but who knows? Narrow though. We'd have to carry our packs. Shall we?"

With difficulty they edged crabwise. Contrary to their expectations the passage continued beyond the bounds of the small cave.

"You alright?" panted Mick.

"This squeezing's making me claustrophobic," wheezed Dave.

"Hang on, it's getting wider now. Yes, here we go! We can turn and walk forwards now."

"What a relief," sighed Dave. "I've had nightmares like that. How did you spot the gap in the first place?"

"A sheer fluke. I was standing at an angle when I shone my torch into the cave. It would have been impossible to see it otherwise."

The passage began to widen a little more so that eventually they were walking comfortably side by side and were able to put their backpacks on again.

"I can't quite believe this is happening," said Mick in a voice which was beginning to echo. "Hear that?"

"Yes, an echo. That means we're coming to – good lord, and there it is. Another cave. Can you believe this?"

The excited men emerged from the passage into another cave a little bigger than the first. They took off their backpacks, found their lamps and gazed around.

"Not much different from Omar's cave," said Mick, flashing his torch around the walls. "No obvious outlets to other chambers. Nothing remarkable about the ceiling…"

"Hallo, what's that?" interrupted Dave, shining his torch towards the wall on their far right. "Look – there's something odd about that bit of wall."

The men went over to where the wall ended. What they saw rendered them silent for a few moments. Mick whistled between his teeth. "Someone's been here before," he said in a voice of suppressed excitement.

Dave's hand was on the wall. "Slabs of stone. Properly dressed stone cut into regular shapes." He turned to look at Mick. "What have we got here?"

"I think my knees have turned to jelly," said Mick.

They were looking at what appeared to be a construction of stone slabs piled systematically one upon another, as though an opening in the cave wall had been bricked up – the original opening having been about two feet wide and six feet high.

"Well," said Dave, trying to control his excitement, "having come this far we must try to find out what's behind here." He went to his backpack and returned with a small metal pick.

"What do you think you're going to do with that?"

"It's dry-stone walling, isn't it?" said Dave. "What's been piled up can be unpiled."

Dave knocked against one of the slabs with the pick. "Hear that?"

"Yes. It's hollow behind there. The plot thickens." Mick's voice was unsteady. "How about trying to dislodge one of the top ones."

Dave reached up and carefully inserted the pointed side of the pick between the top left slab and the natural rock wall. He jiggled the metal point until he thought he had achieved purchase, and then gave a gentle tug. He shook his head. "Tight as a drum. I don't want to do any damage. Whoever built this wall knew what they were doing."

"We've got to get in there somehow. I'm going to fetch a hammer." Mick strode to his backpack and came back carrying the hammer.

"We don't want to split any of these stones," said Dave anxiously, noting the stubborn expression on his friend's face. "Let's take it easy, right?"

"OK. Put the pick in again and I'll tap it."

Reluctantly Dave inserted the metal point. Mick began to tap, cautiously at first, then a little harder.

After a few moments, Dave shouted, "Stop! Something moved!" He began to jiggle the pick again, then pulled. The slab began to move outwards towards them. "Can we just stop a minute? My heart's jumping around like a jack-in-the-box."

"So's mine," admitted Mick. "Right now I'd give anything for a cool glass of Guinness."

"Give me a gin and tonic with a slice of lemon and I'm anybody's," added Dave with feeling. "Whoever built this wall was a craftsman. The slabs are exactly the same size and the whole thing fits. Right, shall we get this one out of the wall?"

Gradually the slab slid forward. When it was almost out, Dave dropped the pick and put both his hands around the slab. He pulled gently and then he was suddenly holding the slab which was about one inch high and roughly six inches square. They looked at each other, and then up at the dark space where the slab had been.

"Oh my God," whispered Dave, "what have we found?"

"Look at the natural rock above," said Mick. "It's been worked to accommodate the evenness of the slabs. How could they have done that?"

Carefully, and in a state of controlled excitement, they removed slabs and piled them meticulously in order on the floor, until they had rendered the wall low enough to peer over the top.

"You look first, milord," said Dave.

Mick, being the shorter of the two, stood on tiptoe and shone his torch downwards. There was a tense silence, and then Mick spoke in a quiet and unsteady voice. "Remember Howard Carter? Tutankhamen?"

Dave drew a sharp intake of breath.

"A gleam of gold. Can't make out what it is – we'll have to take out a few more slabs."

Mick stepped back. "Take a look."

Dave approached the wall and shone his torch downwards. He looked in silence and then stepped back. "Can we rest for a minute or two? My heart's racing so fast I can hardly breathe."

They sat on the floor of the cave. After a few moments, Dave said, "It's big, it's gold, and it's just got to be the 'Terrible Treasure' the last custodian mentioned."

"Why terrible?" said Mick. "And why do we have to veil our faces before we look, unless it's radioactive or something?"

"Perhaps it's to preserve whatever it is from contamination, like human breath."

"Come on, let's take the slabs down to a level where we can see the thing properly. I'm trying to imagine what Omar's face would have looked like if he'd seen it."

"I wish the slabs weren't quite so heavy," said Dave, trying to sound grumpy to steady his nerves.

They worked steadily until the level had been reduced to chest height, a labour which helped calm their emotions. Mick stepped back and gave a theatrical bow.

"Your turn for first go, milord."

Dave approached the wall, took a deep breath and shone the torch downwards. For a moment there was silence, then, "Just hand me one of the lamps, will you?"

Mick obliged and Dave gave a loud cry – almost a scream. He staggered backwards, dropped the torch, then still gripping the lamp he sagged to his knees. Mick rushed to his aid, took the lamp from him and caught him as he crumpled sideways.

"What the hells' the matter with you, man?" Anxiety made Mick's voice terse. "Did something happen when you looked?"

Dave, was lying on his back and shaking violently. He simply raised one hand and pointed to the partly demolished wall.

Mick picked up the lantern and approached the wall nervously, wondering why the cuneiform tablet had spoken of the 'Terrible Treasure' and feeling cold sweat running down his back. Amazement rendered him silent.

Dave, still lying on the floor and trembling, turned his head to look at Mick's back. "Tell me what you see," he said hoarsely.

"It's like – a huge gold casket with amazing ornamentation. I can't begin to describe it, except there seems to be two gold winged figures on the top."

"And?"

"It's long, the other end disappears into the darkness to the left. It stands in a small chamber with just a foot or so of clearance either side. How the hell did they get the thing in here? Our wall's far too small." Mick leaned further forward and shone his torch to the left. "Well, I'll be... there's another slab wall just clear of the end of the thing, bigger than ours. That's how they did it. There must be another chamber through there. They've entombed the thing!"

Dave sat up with difficulty and clasped his hands around his knees to control the trembling. "Look down at the feet."

"Feet? There are feet?" Mick shone his torch downwards. "Yes, there they are! How did you..."

"Are there two gold rings, one through each foot?"

"Yes... how the living hell did you know that?"

Dave got slowly to his feet, knees trembling. "I'm a Jew," he said simply. He swayed slightly but managed a lop-sided grin. He picked up a torch and one of the lamps and walked unsteadily to the wall, saying, "I think I'm in shock, but don't worry about it." He drew a deep breath, switched on the torch and held up the lamp. Then he mumbled something in Hebrew and began to cry silently.

Prudently, Mick insisted that they both sat on the floor and rested. "I think I know what we've got here," he said quietly, "but I want to hear it from you."

Dave thought for a moment. "You and I, my friend, have discovered something which has been hidden from the world for around two and a half thousand years. It has shocked me to the core."

"Me too."

"It's fitting that one of us is Jewish. This is the holiest object in the whole of worldwide Judaism. A lost, invisible object the memory of which has always been kept alive."

"I suppose it couldn't be a replica?"

"No way! A replica wouldn't have been sealed up so meticulously. No Mick, the 'Terrible Treasure' of the cuneiform tablet is the Ark Of The Covenant!"

For a few moments they sat in silence. Each tried to come to terms in his own way with the most colossal discovery in archaeology, surpassing even the finding of the tomb of Tutankhamen.

Dave spoke, carefully and with some trepidation. "Of course, you do know our next move, don't you?"

"Try to open it?"

"No, even if that were possible in that restricted space."

"But isn't it supposed to contain the stone tablets of the Ten Commandments?"

"Yes, but we shall never know whether the Babylonians bothered to keep them. Even if they could decipher them, the tablets would have been of no interest to them."

"So what's this next move of ours?"

"To follow the instructions on the cuneiform tablet and seal it up again."

Mick stared unbelievingly at his friend. "What?"

"Believe me, Mick, we can do nothing else."

"You're mad! The greatest archeological find of all time? What are you thinking of, man? We owe it to the world!"

"No. We owe it to the world not to disclose it."

"Why? Why?"

"Let's go back to the sixth century B.C. In 586 B.C. the Babylonians conquered Jerusalem and practically razed it to the ground. They looted every treasure they could get their hands on. It has always been believed that the Ark Of The Covenant was amongst those treasures. They took away treasures and Hebrew captives – 'By the Rivers of Babylon, there we sat down, yea, we wept when we remembered Zion'. Psalm 137. It stands to reason that when they took stolen treasures and captives back to Babylon – modern day Iraq – they would also have carried the Ark there with all the rest of the booty."

"Yes, but what are you getting at?"

Dave sighed. "Why do you think the Ark is referred to as the 'Terrible Treasure'? They knew that the Hebrews would one day have tried to recover it if they knew where it was. It is such a sacred object that many thousands would gladly have died to recover it. The Babylonians had to secrete it somewhere."

"Yes, I understand that, but..."

"So what's changed? I know my people, Mick. Today if they knew it was on Iraqi territory, Islamic territory, they would move heaven and hell to get back their rightful property. On the other hand, Iraq could claim ownership because it was found on their soil. This could blow the Middle East apart. Think about it."

Mick got up and paced about nervously. "Yes, I see your point. But why couldn't it be solved by negotiation?" He intercepted a look from Dave. "Oh yes, there'd be trouble. The fanatics on both sides would make that impossible. *Impasse*. I wish all fanatics were at the bottom of the sea. So what do we do? It seems that we hold the peace of the world in our hands then."

"Exactly so. Maybe we are the 'wise men who could save the world' spoken of in the cuneiform writing – if that isn't too fanciful."

Mick stopped pacing. "If only we had our camera, we could at least have taken photographs."

"No. Not even that."

"Why ever not?"

"If they were to fall by accident into the wrong hands…"

"Got it all worked out, haven't you?" said Mick bitterly.

"Yes. But do you think I'm not agonising at the thought of my people not able to recover the holiest object in the whole of Judaism? I'm dying inside, Mick."

"So the fanatic wins."

"I'm afraid so, and I hate it as much as you do. We can't risk it, Mick." Dave stood up. "Come on, then. We've now got to replace every slab. Remember the writer of the cuneiform tablet saying that we had to 're-seal the place of concealment' once we had looked at the 'Terrible Treasure'."

"So what are we going to tell Omar when we visit him in hospital?"

"Same thing we are going to tell the Iraqi officials when we get back – we came away with nothing. It will be the truth. Now let's seal it up again before I weaken."

"OK," said Mick, getting to his feet. "If we must, we must – only let's get on with it. I shall hate every slab I put back."

"Do you mind waiting a moment? There's something I have to do first," said Dave, standing and exploring his backpack.

Mick watched as Dave drew out a small black decorated skullcap and fitted it to his head. Dave then walked over to the treasure chamber and bent to touch the sacred object. His hand connected with one of the winged figures. He began to chant softly in Hebrew, making a slight rocking motion. The sight brought a lump to Mick's throat.

As Dave walked back to him, Mick said, "I don't know what those gold rings are doing on each foot."

"Didn't those monks at your old school in Ireland teach you anything about religion?" said Dave with a tired smile.

"Of course they did, but it was mostly New Testament, not so much the Old."

"Those rings are on all four feet. Poles or staves were pushed through the rings and that's how the Ark was lifted and carried about. It's said that sometimes the Ark was carried into battle."

"With what purpose?"

"Now you've got me. I've never found out. Come on, let's get started or we'll be here all night."

***

"After all our precautions the Middle East is in a packet of trouble anyway," said Mick, draining his whisky glass. "Have another Irish?"

Dave shook his head. "I'm still waiting to hear why you got in touch with me after all these years. Not that it isn't good to see you."

Mick poured himself another whisky before replying. He looked at his old friend with a strange expression which filled Dave with foreboding. "I'm dying, Dave," he said. "No, don't say anything. What can you say? I have only months, maybe weeks. I need to give you something."

"I think I will have that other whisky," said Dave. "So what do you want to give me?"

Mick pushed the bottle towards Dave. "Help yourself. Now listen. You remember I had mixed feelings about sealing up the chamber?"

Dave nodded, feeling a sudden stab of anxiety.

"Well, many years ago I wrote our book."

"What book?"

"The book which you and I should have written together. I knew you would have nothing to do with it, so I wrote our story by myself."

Dave had gone pale. "I take it that it's unpublished?"

"Of course."

"Then why write it?"

"I had a compulsion to do it. I did a little more research on the subject and found out that the original container was a wooden box made of acacia wood, when I had imagined that the whole thing was solid gold."

Dave nodded. "That's right. It was gold plated on the inside and the outside and then ornamented."

"Now I want you to have the manuscript. Do whatever you like with it. I'm beyond involvement now."

Mick leaned sideways, pulled out a large brown envelope from a drawer and pushed it toward Dave. "This is the only copy in existence.

I've wiped it from my computer. I want you to take it back to Shropshire with you."

Dave touched the envelope. "So it's all in here? Everything?"

"Everything."

Dave looked thoughtfully at the envelope. "Are you sure you want me to have it?"

Mick shrugged and gave a grin which brought back something of his younger self. "I can hardly take it with me, can I?"

"Suppose I burnt it with the autumn leaves in my back garden?"

A spasm passed across Mick's face. "That's entirely up to you, of course."

Dave gazed down at the envelope, remembering. "I hope with all my heart that nobody will ever discover our treasure."

"I think it highly unlikely. They would have to find two optical illusions first, wouldn't they? First they would have to be in the exact spot at the time the setting sun sculpted the evening frog boulder for a few moments, then they would have to spot the gap in the wall."

"We managed it, didn't we?"

"A sheer fluke. If I had been standing a few inches to the left my torch would never have picked up that oddity. A chance in a million."

Dave sighed. "The Middle East is now in great turmoil. This story going public would be like pouring paraffin on an inferno. Alright, I'll take it home and think about it."

"That's all I ask."

Their parting was emotional. Fortunately there was nobody in Dave's railway carriage at first. There was just enough time for a few tears to dry before the carriage filled.

***

Rooks were cawing in the nearby woods. The sun was close to setting and the air was filled with the smell of burning autumn leaves. Dave steadily raked more into heaps, ready to fling them onto the fire. When the blaze was hot enough he bent and picked up a large brown envelope, gazed at it for a long moment, then pushed it with the rake into the hottest part of the fire.

"Goodbye, old friend," he muttered. "Forgive me for destroying your testimony, but this could save many lives."

"David! Dinner in ten minutes!" called a woman's voice from the house.

The rooks cawed; the sun set. The Ark Of The Covenant slept in its tomb.

Miss Henshaw, Paracelcus and Khubla Khan

The elderly woman pushing the magazine-and-drinks trolley stood quietly aside as the doctor, consulting his list, spoke to the nurse.
"And who has been admitted to this side ward?"
"Agnes Henshaw, doctor. Came in last night. Terminal, I'm afraid."
"Age?"
"One hundred and one."
The doctor whistled under his breath and the pair went into the side ward, leaving Edith King looking after them thoughtfully as she stood still and remembered. Henshaw? Agnes Henshaw? She looked back over her shoulder at the door of the ward, oddly named 'Paracelcus', and then continued on her way to the main ward.

***

Edith King, fourteen years old, blonde, brown-eyed and small for her age, sat at the back of the classroom waiting for her idol to arrive and give Edith's favourite lesson – English Literature. Hunger, always in the background, receded when Miss Henshaw was holding her class spellbound.

Edith was hungry because she was a war-time evacuee living in a household where she was given only the minimum amount of food to keep her going – never enough to satisfy the ill-timed adolescent burgeoning of her appetite. She would doodle in the margins of her exercise books, drawing steaming plum puddings, whole roasted chickens, iced cakes and bowls overflowing with fruit. At night she would dream of her mother's feather-light Yorkshire puddings and crisp roast potatoes, delicious stews and apple pie with thick creamy custard. She could no longer remember the taste of bananas. If there was ever any exotic fruit around it was exclusively for the under-fives. The urgent appetites of growing schoolchildren were not considered as priority by the war-time coalition cabinet and many children had been alloted unlucky billets.

The true story of the evacuation scheme – well-meant but all too often handled with appalling insensitivity – was never to be told in full. Billeting officers seldom made follow-up visits to see that all was well, and children who had been brought up in the 1930's did not have the self-confidence to complain to adults. If there had been such a thing as a medal for sheer endurance, thousands of evacuees would have qualified. They would have had no way of knowing that a lifetime later there would be a gathering of tearful elderly ex-evacuees at a service in Westminster Abbey, to recognise at last that children too had played their part in the war effort – in their own nightmare of being taken from their homes and given like parcels into the care or otherwise of strangers, some of whom were deeply resentful of this intrusion into their homes. The children could not have known that during the Abbey Service all those years later, two Spitfire aircraft would execute a fly-past over the Abbey solely in their honour. A splendid gesture, but half a century too late to wipe out the life-long emotional scars still resonating in the nervous systems of a large part of the population. Others had experienced far worse during the Second World War, but children had carried and grown old with their own sad secrets.

Edith looked through the classroom window at the sky and thought that the billowing clouds look like piles of buttery mashed potatoes. She pushed her fist against her stomach and looked away.

Miss Henshaw bustled into the room, her spectacles as usual slipping down her short nose. She was a round little person, bland-faced with bright blue intelligent eyes. In the street nobody would have given her a second glance, yet as she arrived the whole room became charged with a kind of electric energy. The girls rose politely.

"Sit down, girls," said the small woman with a keen look around at the faces. The Lower Fourth were her favourites, especially one girl. Edith King was beginning to develop in English lessons in a most interesting way. A pity she was so hopeless at mathematics and so useless at games. Miss Henshaw cast a quick glance at Edith's pale face and remembered seeing her yesterday coming away from the hockey field, breathless and trembling with fatigue, and thinking that the child did not seem well – in contrast to the others who were bright-eyed and rosy with the excitement of the game.

"Today," said Miss Henshaw, "we will continue with the Lake Poets. Before that, I would like you to consider how rich our language is. Take a few moments to think of your favourite words, then I will ask you each in turn to tell me two of them."

Words tumbled around in Edith's mind like a kaleidoscope. They scintilated like a shower of stars, she almost saw them glittering in the air around Miss Henshaw's neat brown hair.

One by one the girls stood and delivered words until it came to Edith's turn. Although she dreaded the ordeal of speaking in class, she had finally managed to make her choice.

"Gossamer – and sheen," she said in her usual self-effacing whisper.

"Speak up, Edith. I couldn't hear."

"Gossamer and sheen. And hundreds more."

"Two will do nicely, thank you." The rest of the class giggled and Edith flushed. "I'm beginning to think that there's something rather interesting developing with you, Edith."

The other girls sniggered behind their hands and nudged each other – hockey girls, netball girls, tennis girls, popular girls who flocked together within their own exclusive circles. The pantomime did not go unnoticed by Miss Henshaw, who said quickly, "And congratulations on your essay, Edith. I'll see you afterwards about it. Now, kindly open your poetry books on Page twenty-four."

***

Edith sat drinking coffee in the hospital canteen, gazing down into the car park and a group of trees and shrubs beyond. Birds flittered about the treetops and the glass and metal of the cars glittered in the hot sunshine. Edith was acutely aware that Paracelcus Ward was immediately above her. Finally she made a decision, pushed away her half-empty cup and purposefully left the canteen to find the nearest lift.

"Yes?" said the ward sister as Edith knocked at the open door of the office. "Oh, hello Edith."

Edith hesitated, feeling her heart beating a little faster. "Er... why is this ward called Paracelcus?" she asked, stalling for time. "I wonder about it every time I push my trolley past."

"That's something I'm always being asked. Well, apparently back in the sixteenth century there was some old alchemist who was into magic, science, medicine etc. His name was – wait for it! – Theophrastus Philipus Aurelius Bombastus von Hohenheim. He called himself Paracelcus, I think after an ancient Roman called Celcus so he must have thought a lot of himself. A rich philanthropist had written a book about him called 'Paracelcus'. He donated all the equipment in this ward. The hospital wanted to name the ward after him, but he insisted they named it after old Theo."

"Oh, right."

The sister looked closely at Edith. "There's something else?"

"Yes." Edith took a deep breath. "I think I know the patient in Paracelcus."

"Oh? Friend of yours?"

"Not exactly. And it's only a hunch, although the age would be right. Might not be her at all."

"Would you like it to be?"

"I would."

"Then why don't you slip in and take a look? She'll probably be asleep but you might be lucky. She's on the way out, I'm afraid, but she sometimes rallies amazingly."

"Thanks."

Edith stood for a moment outside the open door of the side ward, and then went in. She lifted a small chair to the bedside, not looking at the still outline of the patient, sat down and put her hand to her throat to calm herself. Slowly she turned her head and looked down at the sleeping face.

***

After morning prayers the headmistress held up her hand for silence.

"Before you go to your classes there is something I must say. It has come to my notice that some of you girls are in the habit of wandering along country lanes at weekends, picking and eating nuts and berries. Hedge nuts are all very well, but as far as berries are concerned this must stop. You are townbred children, not country bred. You may not be sure of what you are eating and you could well poison yourselves. Please desist from this dangerous habit. Anyone seen doing it will be reported to me. Thank you, that is all."

Edith felt herself blushing a deep red, partly from guilt and partly from anger at having been deprived of a supplement to her meagre diet. She and a small group of others had indeed been the culprits, all from billets where they were ill-fed and made to feel like interlopers living on charity.

Happily the morning began with English Literature that day. Edith forgot her anger and her hunger as Miss Henshaw began to read aloud.

> "In Xanadu did Khubla Khan
> A stately pleasure dome decree
> "Where Alph, the sacred river, ran
> "Through caverns measureless to man
> "Down to a sunless sea."

The words, delivered with a touch of magic from a brilliant teacher, riveted Edith's attention and caused ripples of sensation along her spine. All that day, and for days afterwards, snatches of Coleridge's mystical and probably drug-induced poem spoke to a kind of echo-chamber deep inside her, which colour-washed her thinking processes. She flowed with the sacred river through the measureless caverns, she breathed the perfume of the incense-bearing trees, she drank the milk of Paradise. She almost forgot to think about food or to worry about her parents being in deadly danger, night after night in the London blitz.

About a year later she wrote a desperate letter to her parents pleading to be allowed to come home. It was finally arranged for her to go back and join the school in London, where many schools had re-opened to accommodate the numbers of evacuees who had drifted back for various reasons. The bombing terrified her, but it was infinitely preferable to the nightmare of evacuation. The plump child of eleven who was sent away in confused and emotional turmoil was very different from the thin anxious girl of fifteen with the haunted eyes who came back. Her mother's clever ways with food rationing put back some of the lost weight, but Edith and her parents had to get to know each other all over again. Although Edith hoped that Miss Henshaw would join the teachers who were also beginning to return, she never saw her again.

Edith eventually left school after the war to enter a tedious and mind-numbing world of office work – but with a precious legacy. A deep love of English writers and poets, leading to the exploration of foreign writers, enriched her mind and was a source of endless pleasure for the rest of her life, saving her mentality from drowning in the sludge of everyday survival. Too plain to attract the opposite sex and too unsure of herself to make many friends, she had to settle for being single, but a fine teacher's gift had resonated throughout an unremarkable life and Miss Henshaw would live as long as Edith was alive.

***

The seventy-four year old voluntary hospital worker looked down at the shrunken face on the pillow and knew beyond doubt that it was the face of her former mentor. No longer were the cheeks plump and round, but Edith recognised with a leap of the spirit that she was looking at her erstwhile idol. The once-brown hair was now grey and sparse with bald patches; she wore no spectacles, but Edith knew that behind the closed lids the eyes were blue. As she looked down, one of the eyes opened and then closed again.

"Who's that?" said a surprisingly clear voice.

"A friend, I hope."

"What sort of friend? I don't want prayers!"

"You won't get any either."

Then the eyes opened, blue and clear although the surrounding skin was deeply wrinkled. "Well? Introduce yourself then. You don't look like a medical person."

"That's because I'm not, Miss Henshaw."

"Give me my specs, would you?"

Edith picked up a pair of glasses from the top of the locker, leaned forward and placed them gently on the upturned face, remembering with a smile how they had so often slipped down the small nose.

"Thanks, I can see you now." There was a pause, then, "Good lord – Edith King or I'm a Dutchman!"

"You're not a Dutchman."

The two women stared in silence, remembering days long gone as they searched each other's features.

"Rotten war, wasn't it?" said the patient.

"Yes, rotten," said Edith, marvelling at the strength and steadiness of the old lady's voice. "Why did you never come back to the London school? I waited. I wanted more of what you had to give."

The blue gaze grew keener. "And what did I give you, Edith?"

Edith spread her hands in the air with a little gasping laugh. "Where do I begin? Dickens, Thackeray, Shakespeare, Jane Austen, George Eliot, all the Brontës, Kipling, the poets... I could go on."

"Did I really do all that?" The eyes closed again. The old lady murmured, "So long ago – so long..."

A few moments passed in silence and Edith peered down in anxiety, then sat back and waited in case Miss Henshaw had fallen asleep. She's changed so much, Edith thought. So different from the plump little bundle of energy I knew, yet I can still feel something of the old magic coming from her.

A small and incredibly frail hand emerged from beneath the bedclothes, but the eyes were still closed. "Edith?"

"I'm still here." Edith took the extended hand, no barriers remaining of polite and respectful behaviour between teacher and pupil, only two people who had drifted together over an ocean of time.

Miss Henshaw's eyes opened again and she looked up sideways at her visitor, one side of her mouth twisting up into a little smile. "Fancy me recognising you like that, Edith. Quite the old lady yourself now. White hair... used to be yellow. You look good. How old?"

"Seventy-four."

"Good lord – really? Little Edith King? Well, well... I'm over a hundred. Didn't think I'd still be here by now." Miss Henshaw sighed. "All that teaching. All those girls. A lifetime away. What was it all for?"

Edith tightened her grip on the little hand and leaned forward, speaking almost fiercely. "*What was it all for?* I'll tell you. You gave us a thousand doorways into a thousand different worlds. You illuminated those worlds with a kind of magical light. Do you remember reading aloud to us parts of different books? Wuthering Heights? Jane Eyre? Path of The King? Pickwick Papers? And the way you read Keats, Shelley, Coleridge? I particularly remember Khubla Khan. You gave me a love of reading that saved a mundane life from total stagnation. However dull my day might have been, endlessly typing Dear Sir – Yours Faithfully – Dear Sir – Yours Faithfully – I could always come home to my little flat, open any book and enter any world I chose. THAT was what it was all for!"

Edith released the wrinkled hand and sat back, embarrassed at her own outburst.

Miss Henshaw had managed to draw up the other side of her mouth to complete the smile. "Thank you, my dear. How could I have known, all those years ago, that it would be little Edith King who would complete the circle of my life? Yes, perhaps it was worthwhile after all." The old lady seemed lost in thought. "If I did that for you, then perhaps I did it for a few others, do you think?"

"Of course you did. That kind of magic has a resonance, it ripples in waves through minds and must have long-term effects somehow, somewhere."

"There speaks young Edith the essayist – magic, resonance, ripples, waves. You always had a way with words."

"Which you excited in me."

"I expected to see your name amongst books on library shelves, you know."

Edith was silent for a moment, visualising long forgotten piles of rejection letters from publishers. "Oh well," she shrugged, "I'm quite content to plunder the minds of others. There'll always be new books to read. I teach backward children to read in my spare time. It's a joy to see them waking up to the experience. I begin by reading aloud to them and that starts the magic rolling. You see how I steal your own methods? You are still influencing kids' minds through me, aren't you? Maybe that will go rolling on and on through them in the future. And you had the temerity to ask me what it was all for?"

Suddenly Miss Henshaw's wrinkled eyes were full of tears. She put out a hand towards her locker. "Give me one of those tissues, please," she croaked. "See what you've done to me? Now Edith, I'm very tired. I must sleep. Come back and see me again soon. You are better for me than all their drugs."

***

The bedside telephone was ringing. Edith reached for the receiver, noting that it was only 7.30 in the morning.

"Hello Edith. Sorry to wake you so early. I know you like to lie in on your days off." It was the ward sister. "I know you're not on duty today, but could you do me a favour? It's our Miss Henshaw, I don't know what you did to her, but she's taken on a new lease of life. She rallies strongly from time to time, but this is ridiculous! The doctors are amazed – she wasn't supposed to last more than a few days. She keeps asking for you. Says it's urgent. Edith, could you possibly…"

Edith was already out of bed. "Yes, of course. Tell her I'm on my way."

***

Edith knocked on the ward sister's door. "I'm here," she announced. "Never moved so fast in all my life! I'll just pop in and see her now, shall I?"

The sister pointed to a chair. "Sit down, Edith. Thanks for coming, but I'm afraid it's too late. I'm sorry to tell..."

"She's dead, isn't she?" Edith felt as though she had been hit by a wave of freezing water.

"Yes, twenty minutes ago." The sister picked up a piece of paper. "She wrote this for you."

Edith took the paper. The shaky scrawl read: 'You are only in your seventies, a mere babe. Start writing. Do this for me'.

Edith waited until she was safely inside her flat before she broke down. Later that day she systematically destroyed some dusty old manuscripts, then went out and bought several large lined exercise books and some pencils. A long buried urge was beginning to wake up like a trickling excitement, a secret river coursing its way underground to arouse something deep, which had slept for years.

The Birth Of Danny Doubleday

"My dear Dr Penrose, I only asked you because somebody here mentioned that you had a PhD in English Literature."

"My dear Miss Marsh, I haven't read a word of fiction since I left university."

Rhona looked surprised, "Really? Whatever happened? No, don't answer that, it's none of my business."

Philip Penrose took a sip of wine and looked along the table at the other guests who had come to dine with a group of old friends of the host, some of whom were unknown to each other. Sitting next to Philip was Rhona Marsh, a woman in middle age who was a recent addition to the stable of writers under the care of the publisher giving the dinner.

"Motley crew, aren't they?" Philip muttered to Rhona. "Some of them will be writers, of course. Pesky creatures. What are novels but a load of lies anyway? Give me documentaries any day. I don't know how George Pritchard puts up with them."

Rhona emptied her wineglass and put it down with exaggerated care before replying. "I'm a novelist. Mr Pritchard seems to put up with me with remarkable fortitude."

"Oops!" Philip did the only thing he could do in the circumstances. He turned fully to face her and gave her a disarming grin, a ploy which had stood him in good stead many times before. "Foot in mouth in big way. Oh look, your glass is empty. Let me catch the waiter's eye…"

"Oh no, really. If I drink too much my neck goes quite red. Not a pretty sight."

There was silence for a moment, and then Philip said, "To make up for my unfortunate gaff, let me answer your question. I gave up all interest in literature shortly after receiving my doctorate because a girl killed herself over me. We were fellow students and I was quite taken with her at the time. We became an item, as the youngsters say nowadays. We studied together, helped each other. Then the affair tailed off, at least on my part, but not on hers. She knew I was cooling off and she became rather desperate. To cut a long story short, I gained my PhD and she failed. When she took her life I was so sickened that I just wanted to forget the whole university scene and go for something entirely different."

Rhona looked concerned. "What a dreadful thing – I'm so sorry about that. So what did you do eventually?"

"Entered the Civil Service and ended up in Security."

"What – cloak-and-dagger stuff?"

Philip merely smiled and shrugged, then said, "Oh good, here comes dessert. Hope it's not too *nouvelle cuisine*. I'm a solid pudding man myself."

"Then I'm afraid you're doomed to disappointment," said Rhona, having spotted her other neighbour's dessert plate. "It's blackcurrants and an arty crafty swirl of what looks like purple ice cream. Bad luck!"

Philip waved away the offered plate when the waiter came. "No thanks, I'll wait for the cheese."

The waiter bent and whispered into his ear, "Is there anything else we can get you, sir?"

"How about spotted dick and custard?"

A few heads turned hopefully, but the waiter looked offended. "I'm afraid we don't…"

"Never mind, I don't really want dessert anyway."

Rhona had put her napkin to her mouth to prevent herself from giggling. "Oh, well done!" she said as soon as the waiter had withdrawn, "So, if you abandoned literature, what do you do in your spare time? Walk the dog? Watch television? I can't imagine life without books. My flat is lined with them."

"My flat is lined with CD's. Music is my escape. I say, you're not really going to eat that concoction, are you?"

"Just the ice cream. I expect it will give me a purple tongue. As usual with modern cooks, the blackcurrants are as sour as lemons. Why do they never appreciate that blackcurrants are *sharp*? Haven't any of them ever heard of putting sugar with them? Hardly rocket science, is it?"

Philip sighed. "Sugar has been demonised, like salt. Also I'm sure some people think it's posh not to have things very sweet. I tend to scandalise everyone by asking for a sugar sprinkler. Still, we mustn't be ungracious when dear old George there has asked us to dine, must we? Being a bachelor like me, he always gets caterers in with waiters, and ladies wot duz in the kitchen for the washing-up etc, whenever he wants to mix people with different careers. He says the mix makes for interesting conversations. It doesn't always – some you win, some you don't. People like to talk about their own careers with others who already know what they're talking about. It's tedious for a ballet choreographer to explain to a stockbroker exactly what he does."

"Yet here we are, a civil servant and a novelist, and I'm finding this conversation most interesting," said Rhona.

"Gee, thanks," said Philip, putting on an exaggerated American accent. "I take it I'm forgiven for my crassness just now?"

"Forget it. When I said I was a novelist I might have sounded more important than I really am. I have had only one novel published, and Mr Pritchard – George – is pressing me for a two-book contract. I don't want to do that. I think I shall end up being what they called a one-book wonder."

"Why?"

Rhona scooped up the last of her ice cream thoughtfully. "Well… I can't find another idea for a new book. My trouble is that I was overwhelmed by very good reviews in the literary columns; then came the offer of another contract, and all that seemed to kill the writing urge stone dead. It was all so unexpected, you see. I don't think I could handle fame it that ever happened. The thought freezes my blood."

"What was your book about?"

"Oh good – I can't be that well known, then, can I?"

"Have I made another gaff? I'm afraid I don't read literary reviews so I don't know what's going on in the book world."

"OK, I'll tell you what the book is about. It's set in the First World War. A young man goes off to war full of excitement, hardly out of short trousers and games like hiding around street corners and pretending to shoot gangsters or Red Indians. All his thoughts are of glorious heroic deeds, hormones buzzing at the thought of glamorous danger. He comes back with his nerves blasted, a mental and physical wreck. After the war he marries and has a son whom he indoctrinates into being a conscientious objector in the Second World War. The son is killed on the battlefield driving an ambulance. Those are only the bare bones of the story."

"Good lord! I wasn't expecting anything like that."

"I suppose you expected a romance, since I'm female?"

"Touché!"

"Friends told me that the theme was hackneyed, done to death, but Mr Pritchard liked my handling of it and took a chance. Now the film rights have been sold, hackneyed or not."

"Wow! I'm impressed."

"I wish I could be. I'd like to go away to a desert island for a year."

"Would you excuse me for a moment?" said Philip suddenly, glancing at his watch. "I have to make a couple of phone calls. George will think I'm just popping out to the loo. He'd be right, but I'll have my mobile with me."

"Cloak-and-dagger business?"

Philip tapped the side of his nose and stood up. The host called jovially, "That'll cost you a penny, old chap!"

"One of the many inconveniences of getting older, George!" retorted Philip on his way out of the room, whilst the other guests chuckled politely.

When Philip returned the cheese course had arrived, and Rhona was listening with a slightly glazed look and a set smile to a young woman with straight hair, fierce spectacles and no make-up; she was talking in a monotonous voice about the importance of happiness.

"So you see," the young woman finished, "we all have a positive duty to infect others with it."

"Like 'flu?" said Rhona.

The girl gave her a blank look and turned to talk to someone else, whilst Philip gave Rhona a conspiratorial wink, having caught the last of the exchange as he returned.

At the end of the evening, as the guests were saying their goodbyes to the host, Philip managed to catch Rhona as she was leaving. He followed her down the front steps of the house and stopped her on the pavement.

"I say, it looks dangerously like rain. Do allow me to call a cab for you."

"Oh, thanks. Isn't that one coming now?"

The taxi drew up as Philip hailed it. He opened the door and Rhona climbed in. As she sat and began to say goodnight, Philip appeared to freeze and stare through the cab window to the other side of the road.

"Oh my God!" Philip was transfixed in horror.

Rhona looked in the same direction and saw a black car parked on the other side of the road. Two men sat in the front seats, both staring hard at the house. They wore homburg hats pulled well down over their foreheads and their dark coat collars were turned up.

After a moment's hesitation, Philip said urgently, "Quickly – shift up! I'm coming in!"

Rhona only just escaped Philip's bulk enveloping her as he fell into the taxi and slammed the door. He leaned forward and rapped out an address to the driver.

"But – I don't live anywhere near there," objected Rhona, alarmed.

"No. I do."

"But..."

"Please don't ask me to explain right now. I'm being followed." He leaned forward again and said to the driver, "Take another route and make it complicated. I'm trying to shake off that car following us."

"It'll cost yer, squire."

"OK. Understood."

"'Old on to yer 'ats then!" said the driver cheerfully, then gave his passengers a breathtaking helter-skelter ride through London that left Rhona in a daze.

***

Rhona shakily accepted the brandy offered by Philip. She leaned back in the deep armchair and closed her eyes, trying to pull herself together.

"Feeling better now?"

"No." Rhona opened her eyes and gave her host a penetrating look. "That was a most alarming experience. Would you mind explaining what on earth is going on?"

Philip sat down opposite her with his own drink and looked down at his feet for a moment. "I wouldn't know where to begin. Can't tell you much anyway. Sorry about all that pantomime but I might have been in some danger back there."

Rhona sipped her brandy, eyeing him uncertainly. "Are you wanted by the police?"

"Absolutely not. I'm sort of on their side, if you see what I mean."

"Are we back to cloaks and daggers again?"

"Yes."

"Ah." Rhona looked around the room. "I see what you mean about being lined with CD's. But you've got books as well – dozens of them! You lied to me."

"Yes. I get buttonholed by so many people who want to trap me into interminable boring conversations about their own views on literature. Lying defends me."

"And you thought I might be one of them?"

"Well, I didn't know then that you weren't."

Philip got up and crossed to the window, where he carefully moved the closed curtains aside a little. He gave a sharp intake of breath and stepped quickly away.

"What's the matter?"

"I'm afraid our roller-coaster taxi ride was to no avail. Those two guys are parked opposite, sitting there like two black crows. They'll know you're here too."

"Why should they be interested in me?"

"You could be useful to them."

"How?"

"As a hostage."

Rhona nearly dropped her glass. "Dr Penrose, this has gone far enough. Tell me what's going on?"

"I'm afraid I can't do that. I'm bound by the Official Secrets Act. I shall, of course, do my utmost to protect you."

"Oh thanks," said Rhona sardonically. "That makes me feel a whole lot better."

"Do you think you could drop the 'Dr Penrose' now? My name's Philip. As we seem to be in this together, would you tell me your first name?"

"Rhona. And as far as I'm concerned I am 'in' absolutely nothing with you. Now I'd like to use your telephone to call a taxi, please."

Philip sat down again and looked at her anxiously. "I can't allow that. If you took one step outside they'd have you."

Rhona was silent for a moment, trying to think. "They can't sit there for ever. Sooner or later they'll have to eat, find a loo, sleep etc. As soon as they've gone I shall be able to leave. Stands to reason."

"They won't wait that long. They'll find a way into the building somehow."

Rhona was feeling slightly queasy and she put down her brandy unfinished. "If they did get in, what would they do?"

"Shoot me."

"Why?"

"Some years ago I was instrumental in getting those two put away for a very long time. All I can tell you is that it was something to do with undercover work in the Balkans. I was realistic enough to know that sooner or later they would come looking for me. I'm only sorry that you had to get mixed up with it."

"Why do I feel that I'm living in a John Buchan novel?" said Rhona with feeling.

Philip stood up. "I'm going to telephone my superiors. They'll have to sort something out now. Do excuse me, I must make the call in the bedroom. Don't on any account go anywhere near the window!"

Rhona sat rigidly, listening to the muffled sound of Philip's voice from the bedroom. The telephone conversation went on for a long time and Rhona closed her eyes and tried to relax.

She heard a little sound, something between a click and a grating noise, and recognised it with horror as the slow turning of a door handle. Her eyes opened and she saw the door gradually being pushed open. With a shock she saw one of the pursuers standing in the doorway looking directly at her. He gave a slow grin which chilled her blood, turning to speak to someone behind him. Then he stepped into the room, followed by his companion.

At that moment, Philip emerged from the bedroom, relaxed and smiling. "Hi guys!" he said. "Well done – you look a right pair of scoundrels."

"How did we do, Phil?" asked one of the men, removing his black hat.

"Spot on! You nearly frightened *me*."

"I could murder a drink," said the other man, eyeing the brandy. "Lurking with sinister intent is hard work."

Rhona looked from one to the other in bewilderment. "Explain!" she demanded.

"Sit down, everyone," said Philip. He turned to Rhona. "An elaborate little deception, I'm afraid."

"More lies?"

"These are my friends, Brian and Jack. They're actors, and as everyone knows, unemployed actors will do anything if you pay them."

"Watch it, sunshine, or we'll increase our fee," said one of the men.

"Are you telling me," gasped Rhona, "that you put me through all that fright for nothing?"

"Oh no, certainly not for nothing. Do you remember telling me at dinner that you couldn't think of an idea for a new book? Well, I didn't want to see you in the clutches of the dreaded writer's block. I left the table tonight with my mobile to phone these two and the rest you know."

"But all you did was to frighten me to death!"

"Think about it, Rhona. Haven't I just given you the opening pages of your new book? You write it and I can supply background authentically – without of course flouting the sacred Act. We could even collaborate. How about it?"

Rhona was speechless.

***

The book was launched the following spring. It was entitled 'Balkan Vengeance' and was written by Rhona Marsh and Philip Penrose. The hero was a secret agent called Danny Doubleday who was destined to be pitched into further adventures in a dozen future books.

After the launch, Philip and Rhona were dining in a restaurant accompanied by an iced bucket of champagne.

"Tell me something," said Rhona.

"Like what?"

"All those lies you told me. What about the girl who killed herself over you at university? All lies too?"

"No. That was all too true. And it did take me years to open any book of fiction after that."

Philip raised his glass. "Here's to the demise of the one-book wonder."

Rhona raised her glass. "Here's to the birth of Danny Doubleday – even if novels are only a load of lies."

***

Tunnellers and Grobbledingers

Mrs Pargiter went mad on Friday the Thirteenth. If one had to go mad, then Friday the Thirteenth could be the most appropriate day to choose.

Not that the good lady had exactly chosen to go mad that day. It had begun when she was on her knees planting her summer bedding flowers. As she was dropping a sturdy root of Busy Lizzies into the hole which she had just managed to save from the attentions of next door's cat – who had other plans for filling the hole – she thought she heard a knocking sound coming from the potting shed behind her.

Putting down the Busy Lizzie unplanted, she got to her feet with some difficulty, due to her arthritis, and opened the shed door. She blinked around in the dim light from one dusty window. Neat seedlings stood in row on a worktop. Home-grown onions hung in net bags against the walls. Bunches of dried herbs were suspended from various hooks, and the air was disturbed by a continuous knocking noise.

Eventually Mrs Pargiter deduced that the sound was coming from the direction of the floor, and as she looked down she saw one of the wooden floorboards moving. Quickly grasping her late husband's hammer which she kept by the door, she advanced cautiously to where the floorboard was evidently being pounded by something from beneath. Some animal? Escaping underground gas? An unsuspected geyser about to erupt? You never knew with all this global warming. Mrs Pargiter slowly raised the hammer and waited, ready for anything.

The floorboard suddenly splintered upwards, causing Mrs Pargiter to take a backward step. Surely this was no mole or fox? Mrs Pargiter experienced alarm. Then there was a sudden heaving from beneath and from the ensuing jagged hole a small head arose, looked around, saw Mrs Pargiter and screamed. Mrs Pargiter screamed in unison.

The strange little face was about three inches wide, and topped with shaggy rough black hair. The tiny ears were close to the head and came to points at their tops. The deep brown eyes were slanted, almost oriental, and were looking upwards in astonishment.

"Who are you?" said the face fearfully.

Mrs Pargiter stood her ground – after all, whose shed was it? "No, who are you? And what are you doing in my shed?"

The head turned and looked around. "Shed? I'm in a shed?"

"Yes. Mine. What do you mean by breaking through my floor and frightening me to death?"

"*Me*! Frightening *you*! How do you think I feel then, suddenly seeing a creature a mile high towering above me?"

"A mile... I'm only five feet three inches," retorted Mrs Pargiter, holding onto the worktop to support her trembling knees and pushing the hammer against her chest to allay the thumping of her heart. "Do you mind telling me who you are and what you are doing here?"

"I'm Blbry."

"What?"

"Blbry."

"Sounds like bilberry."

"So call me Bill. And what I'm doing here is being lost, that's what I'm doing. I was trying to escape from a grobbledinger."

"What's a grobbledinger?"

"A black horror that eats Tunnellers like me. I wasn't going to be eaten, especially on my birthday."

"Happy birthday."

"Thanks."

"How old are you today?"

"I'm not quite sure. About four hundred and ten, I think."

"Days?"

"No, years."

"But... that would place your birth around the time of Queen Elizabeth the First!"

"Something like that, give or take."

Mrs Pargiter swayed a little and put her hand over her eyes. When she looked again the head was rising, followed by a neck and shoulders, which then became stuck.

"Give me a hand, would you? A huge creature like yourself should be able to pull away some of this broken wood. Ouch! The bits are sticking into me!"

With a trembling hand, but still clutching the hammer with the other, Mrs Pargiter pulled at the splinters until the interloper was freed and was able to scramble up out of the hole in the floor.

The sight which met her eyes robbed her of speech. Before her stood a naked man, thinly covered in black hair. He was about the height of an eighteen month old toddler and muscled like a prize-fighter. Mrs Pargiter blushed, hastily took a blue scarf from her neck and dropping the hammer, flung the scarf around the waist of the little man and knotted it firmly.

Bill stepped back in protest. "Hey! What do you think you're doing?"

"Making you respectable!"

"I've never been respectable in my life!"

"I can see that."

"You've never met a Tunneller before, have you?"

"What's a Tunneller?"

"We live under the ground."

"What, like moles?"

"Yes, and rabbits and badgers. Moles and rabbits are alright, but badgers eat us. Grobbledingers are the worst, though." The little man cast an anxious look at the jagged hole in the floor. "Look, would you mind mending that hole? The grobbledinger who's after me isn't far behind and he might pop up at any minute."

Mrs Pargiter looked around the shed, grabbed the lawnmower and pushed it until it completely covered the hole. "There! I shouldn't think your grobbledinger could shift that. What does a grobbledinger look like?"

"A black slimy thing like a huge slug, all eyes and teeth at one end and a poisonous tail at the other. Here, would you mind lifting me up and sitting me on that table thing up there? I'm getting a crick in my neck looking up at you."

Mrs Pargiter obligingly put her hands under the little man's armpits and lifted him the way she would have lifted one of her grandchildren, seating him on the edge of the worktop. She studied him closely, and he returned an unwinking stare. She noted his long fingernails, like claws.

"Would you like to borrow a nail file?"

"Whatever for?"

"You'll never be able to play the piano with fingernails like that."

"I haven't got a piano."

"So why do you need such long fingernails?"

Bill eyed her scornfully. "You do ask a lot of silly questions, don't you? We are *Tunnellers*. We *dig* our way around, and to do that we need scraping claws. We tunnel our way everywhere underground, and we scrape out great caverns and halls to live in. You wouldn't believe the network of tunnels beneath your feet. Way down, of course, or your builders and roadmakers would discover us. If we build too high up we could shift your foundations."

"But... that could make our buildings unsafe, couldn't it?"

"So what do you suppose happened to the leaning tower of Piza?"

By now Mrs Pargiter was beginning to think that she must either be in a nightmare and would soon wake up, or she was losing her mind. She settled for losing her mind, and to steady her nerves she asked another question.

"All this scraping you do – what happens to all that soil you dig out?"

Bill gave her a sly grin, making him resemble a garden gnome. "We throw it upwards. We leave it around in mounds in woodlands, in fields, sometimes on people's lawns. They wouldn't know the difference between molehills and our rubbish."

"What? On our lawns? That's very inconsiderate." Mrs Pargiter unfolded a garden chair and sat down, as her trembling knees were beginning to feel quite frail. "Tunnellers... grobbledingers... what next, I wonder?"

"You people can't see us, you know."

"What? So who am I looking at right now, then?"

"Well, normally we're invisible to you. That is, if we're in good health. If not, something goes wrong and people see us then, so we have to be very careful to keep out of sight. Usually we can dance around you and pull faces and you wouldn't suspect a thing if we're quiet. The trouble is..." and here Bill's eyes filled with tears, "...I'm not very well."

Immediately Mrs Pargiter forgot her nerves and took out a pocket handkerchief. She reached up, pulled Bill down from the worktop and sat him on her lap, drying his eyes and stroking his rough black hair. He smelled just like the earth she had been digging to put her plants in.

"What's the matter with you, then?" she asked. "Can I give you an aspirin?"

Bill shook his head. "I was bitten by an adder a few months ago and I haven't been very well since. I'm so tired I just want to go to sleep all the time." He leaned his head against Mrs Pargiter's ample bosom and whimpered. Mrs Pargiter's motherly soul was awakened.

"I know just what you need."

"What?"

"A good long rest and feeding up."

"Do I?"

"Yes. Come on!"

She stood him on the floor, got stiffly to her feet, then bent to pick up the small creature and carried him like a human child back into her cottage – after a cautious look around at the neighbouring windows.

Once indoors, she carried him upstairs and took him into what had once been her son's bedroom. The bed was already made up as her grandson often came to stay for weekends, not liking to go fishing with his father. She sat Bill in a chair while she pulled back the bedclothes and plumped up the pillows, feeling that she was being useful once more.

Bill stared around the room in wonder. "I've never been inside one of your caverns before. It's amazing!"

"It's not a cavern, it's a house."

"Yeah, whatever."

"Now," said the lady firmly, "you are not getting into this nice clean bed in that state." She took a clothes brush from the dressing table, stood Bill on the floor and began vigorously to brush away the soil clinging to him.

"Hey – that hurts!" objected Bill, trying to wriggle out of her grasp. "I'm always covered in soil, it's my natural state. Leave off!"

"That will do, I suppose, although I'd much rather give you a good bath."

"Oh no you won't! That's disgusting! Only dirty people have to bath. Nice clean soil keeps us fresh all the time."

In one quick movement, Mrs Pargiter picked up Bill and put him in the bed, propping him up against the pillows. Immediately Bill's attitude changed. He leaned back with half-closed eyes like a sleepy cat, an expression of pure joy on his face.

"Oh boy, this is heaven," Bill purred. "It's all so soft, so smooth. We don't have anything like this underground." His eyelids drooped and in seconds he was fast asleep.

Mrs Pargiter tiptoed away to the kitchen and opened a tin of tomato soup, not sure what Tunnellers ate. As the soup was heating on the hob, she searched around in cupboards until she found the smallest bowl she possessed, one she usually kept odds and ends in, like safety pins and paper clips. *That'll do for soup*, she thought, picking up a round coaster which would serve as a tiny plate for bread and finding the smallest spoon in the cutlery drawer.

A little later she was climbing the stairs carrying a small round tray normally used for sherry glasses. On it was tastefully arranged the bowl of soup, the little coaster with a piece of bread, and the spoon. A folded handkerchief tissue served as a napkin.

She put the tray down on the dressing table and turned to the bed. There was no Bill lying back on the pillows. Surprised by the intensity of her feelings of disappointment, she ran to the open window and looked down into the garden, but there was no sign of her visitor. *Right – I'm barmy. I imagined it all*, she thought. Then she heard a snore.

Looking at the bed she saw a small hump in the centre. She pulled the bedclothes back and disclosed the little man curled up in a tight little ball.

"Wake up, Bill – you'll suffocate!"

"What? Oh, hallo. I dropped off."

Mrs Pargiter hauled him back to the pillows. "What on earth were you doing down there?"

"Resting my eyes from the light. Don't get too much of that, being underground. Takes getting used to."

"So how do you manage to see at all down there?"

"Simple. We put our headlights on."

"Headlights? Where do you get them from?"

"Nowhere. They're built in. Watch this."

Mrs Pargiter saw a white glow beginning in the middle of Bill's forehead. It grew in intensity, and then began to fade away.

"See? Headlights. We're born with them."

Mrs Pargiter put her hand over her eyes for a moment, feeling in a state of unreality, then she pulled herself together and fetched the tray to the bed.

"Now sit up straight and have this tray on your knees. This is the beginning of you getting better – good food."

"What's this then?" said Bill, sniffing suspiciously at the bowl.

"Tomato soup."

"Oh good, I like tomatoes."

"You have *tomatoes* under the ground?"

Bill looked up at her with another sly grin, making him look more than ever like a garden gnome. "Pinch them from your gardens, don't we? And lettuces. And carrots. And we nibble around your cabbages. I'll bet you blame things like slugs and caterpillars."

Bill began to slurp his soup with satisfaction, eventually abandoning the spoon and drinking the dregs from the bowl. "Scrumptious!" he said with relish. "Anything else?"

"Tinned rice pudding."

Suddenly the doorbell rang.

"Quick!" hissed Mrs Pargiter. "Hide under the bedclothes. Take the tray and things with you. Try not to suffocate. I'll get rid of whoever it is."

She opened the front door to see her grandson Jimmy looking up at her.

"Guess what, Gran?" said the child in some excitement. "We've just been watching one of those antique telly shows."

"What, like Dad's Army?"

"No, not old shows – about antiques like old vases and stuff. Someone's just made a bomb in the auction, selling a pile of old comics!"

"Oh good," said Mrs Pargiter absently, casting a nervous glance over her shoulder at the staircase.

"And Dad says there's a stack of his grandad's old comics on the top shelf of the wardrobe in his old room. Let's go up and find them!"

Jimmy pushed past his grandmother and darted towards the stairs.

"No, wait!" cried Mrs Pargiter, causing Jimmy to pause at the foot of the stairs. "Let's go into the kitchen first and have milk and chocolate cakes. You like your Gran's cake, don't you?"

"Not now, Gran. Come on!" Jimmy pounded up the stairs. Mrs Pargiter followed as fast as her stiff joints would allow.

Once in the bedroom, Mrs Pargiter saw with relief that Jimmy had opened the wardrobe door and was looking up at the high shelf. She went quickly to a chest of drawers and began to pull out clothes, scarves, tablecloths, anything which came to hand, and to fling them all on to the bed in a jumbled heap.

"What are you doing that for, Gran?" said a puzzled Jimmy.

"I was just about to tidy up all these drawers when you rang the bell."

"Never mind about all that, Gran. Look up there! I can see the cardboard box Dad told me about. Can you get it down for me?"

"Good heavens, is that still there? Well, it's much too high for me to reach. We'll wait until your Dad can come round, shall we?"

"No way, Gran. Get your kitchen steps. I want to see those comics. You wouldn't believe what that lot on the telly sold for!"

"Alright, let's go down together then. You can help me carry the steps."

There was a muffled sneeze. Quickly Mrs Pargiter pulled out her handkerchief and dabbed ostentatiously at her nose. "Hope I'm not starting a cold," she muttered.

Between them they brought up the steps and set them up beside the wardrobe, but not before Mrs Pargiter had noticed that two jumpers, three pillow cases and a squashed hat had somehow got themselves on to the floor.

"Must have slipped off the bed," she said lamely, and picked up the articles and slammed them back on the bed. A little squeak was heard, which the lady covered with a cough.

"Will you go up or me?" said Jimmy.

"You. I'll hold the steps steady. Up you go – be careful now!"

Willingly Jimmy scrambled up the steps and handed the box down to his grandmother. Then he jumped to the floor, grabbed the box and sat on the bed with a heavy bounce. There was another squeak.

"Oh, those old bedsprings! I really must oil them," simpered Mrs Pargiter.

Jimmy tore off the lid and looked eagerly inside. "Yes! Yes yes yes! The Dandy! The Beano! Just like on the telly!"

He bounced up and down on the bed squealing with delight, fortunately covering other sounds from beneath the pile of clothes.

"Jimmy dear, get up please. You're creasing all those things."

"OK. I'm taking this lot home to show Dad." Jimmy slid off the bed and darted to the door, calling back over his shoulder. "I'll let you know if we're millionaires!"

Mrs Pargiter listened until she heard the front door bang and Jimmy's feet pounding along the garden path, then she pulled the jumbled clothes to the floor and jerked back the bedclothes.

Bill slowly emerged, his shaggy hair standing on end and a furious expression on his little face. "What the hell's been going on? I've been squashed to death! I'm bruised all over! I thought you were supposed to be looking after me?" He reached beneath the bedclothes and pulled out tray, coaster, bowl and spoon and flung them to the floor. "And all these nasty hard things have been cutting into me every time that creature bounced!"

"That creature happens to be my grandson. I'm sorry he bounced, but there was nothing I could do." Mrs Pargiter sat Bill up against the pillow. "Now how would you like some nice rice pudding?"

"Right now nice rice pudding would make me sick. I'm bruised and battered. How about an aspirin?"

Mrs Pargiter went to the bathroom and came back with an eyebath of water and just a small piece of aspirin, in view of Bill's size. When he had swallowed the aspirin, with much grumbling about the revolting taste, he lay back on the pillow and looked pathetic.

Mrs Pargiter sat on the edge of the bed.

"Hey, don't you squash me!" cried Bill anxiously.

"Don't be silly, I'm nowhere near you. Bill, tell me something."

Bill closed his eyes wearily. "What? I can't think too clearly right now."

"About the way you talk. If you're four hundred and odd years old, shouldn't you be talking like Shakespeare?"

"No."

"But you were born four centuries ago, yet you talk like a street-wise youngster of today."

Bill sighed. "Think about it," he said. "Nothing stays the same forever, and that includes language. We go about amongst you so often that we pick up on the way you talk. Once I might have said 'Prithee cast thine eye on yonder beauteous rose'. Now I'd say, 'Hey, look at that lovely rose'. Another time I might have said 'Gadzooks!' or 'Odds boddikins!' Now I'd probably say, 'Bloody hell' or something . See?"

"Oh. Right. That clears that up then." She stood up. "Now you snuggle down and go to sleep, and I'll go downstairs and cook something nice for your dinner."

"That tomato soup was nice."

"Yes, but you need something solid. I was thinking about shepherd's pie, or casseroled beef and dumplings. Or what about cod and chips?"

But Bill was fast asleep.

***

As Bill's health improved day by day, he began to become rather misty around the edges. Soon Mrs Pargiter could see right through him. One day, as she came into his bedroom with his egg-cup of morning coffee – a beverage he was fast becoming addicted to – she saw a lump beneath the bedclothes but no Bill. With a lurch of the heart she knew that her little visitor was completely cured.

The bedclothes stirred and the dent in the pillow shifted.

"Don't look so alarmed," said Bill calmly. "I'm still here. Just give me my coffee."

"Where's your hand then?"

"Don't worry, I'll take it from you."

The egg-cup was taken, seeming to float through the air towards the pillow, and then was drained.

"Ta," said Bill, and the egg-cup came back towards the lady.

Mrs Pargiter plucked it delicately from the empty air, then sat on the bedside chair feeling sad and troubled.

"You're better now, aren't you, Bill?" she said tentatively.

"Yes," replied Bill in what Mrs Pargiter thought was an unnecessarily cheerful tone. "You're a dam' fine nurse. Can't see me at all now, can you?"

"No."

"So you know I'll have to go home today, don't you?"

"I suppose so. Will I ever see you again?"

"Maybe, if I get ill again. Tell you what – why don't you leave that hole in the floor of your shed, then I can come and visit you any time I like."

"Suppose the grobbledinger comes up through it?"

"He won't. Grobbledingers hate coming up to the surface unless they think they can catch something nice to eat – like me. They can't stand the daylight."

"But if you visit me I won't be able to see you, will I? Unless you get flu or something nasty."

"No, but that won't stop us talking, will it?"

Mrs Pargiter smiled. "Of course not. Oh, I should like that, Bill. Do please promise that you'll come."

"You got it!"

"There you go again, street-wise talking." Mrs Pargiter sighed. "I've really enjoyed these last few days. I've missed having someone to look after. And you will be able to tell me all about those historic days you've lived through."

"Cool!"

***

Later that afternoon Mrs Pargiter, after making sure that nobody was looking out of neighbouring windows, followed a blue scarf as it floated a little above the garden path towards the shed. Once inside, the scarf paused by the lawnmower.

"Come on, then – shift this thing out of the way," came Bill's voice.

Mrs Pargiter reluctantly heaved the lawnmower aside, revealing the jagged hole.

"What's your name?" Bill unexpectedly asked.

"Jenny."

"Well then, Jenny, this is goodbye. Thank you for making me better. No, don't cry. You know I'll be back."

Suddenly the blue scarf detached itself and floated towards her. She bent to take it and dried her eyes with it. "Goodbye Bill. When you come back, what would you like for dinner?"

"Bangers and mash and tinned rice pudding!" came Bill's voice, but this time it sounded further away. In fact, from down the hole.

Mrs Pargiter stepped to the hole and bent down. "Bill? Are you still there?" She reached down the hole and felt around. "Bill?"

But Bill had gone home.

***

Later that day her daughter-in-law rang to ask her what she would like for her approaching birthday. Glancing through the window towards the garden shed, she considered for a moment before saying, with a secret smile, "Well dear, I think I would really love a nice little garden gnome."

If Mrs Pargiter had really gone mad, at least nobody would ever know about it.

Lady Of Secrets

"Giacomo!" The voice of the master rang through the twilit house. "Where are you, boy?"

"Here," called a young man's voice from another room, "overseeing your supper."

"Leave that to the servants and bring candles – lamps – anything to give me light!"

A handsome youth appeared in the doorway and peered disapprovingly at the man sprawled in a chair with hands clasped under his chin, whilst gazing unblinkingly at a portrait on an easel.

"You can't eat candles. You have eaten nothing all day. Let me attend to supper and then I'll bring lamps. There's light enough."

"It's too dark to see her face properly. Bring lights and don't argue with me, Master Salai."

"No – supper first," retorted the lad firmly. "You'd waste away if I didn't look after you."

The man grabbed a book from a table at his elbow and threw it at Giacomo, who merely dodged gracefully and disappeared through the doorway, calling as he went, "And when are we going to Milan again? I want to visit my old home!"

"Never, if you don't do as you're told."

The boy's head re-appeared around the doorway. "Does that mean we might be going?"

"Light! Lights!"

The head withdraw and the man resumed his concentrated stare until the boy arrived with a flickering candelabra, which caused the painting on the easel to come alive.

"And now supper," said the boy crossly as he hurried back to the kitchen.

The man drew a deep breath before speaking in a throaty whisper. "My Lady of Secrets... the boy doesn't know you. How could he? To him you are just another wife of a wealthy man who is anxious to record his lady's beauty for posterity. Only I in the whole world know what you know, see what you see with those speaking eyes. Forgive his ignorance."

The young man bustled in and out with plates, knives, baked meats, bread and wine, finishing with a small basket of fruit, all of which he placed on the table next to the man's chair. He then drew up a stool and sat, beginning to carve the meat.

"No meat. Give me bread and fruit," said the man, never taking his eyes from the painting. "Oh, and wine. Let us drink to our safe journey to Milan."

The man's young companion nearly dropped his knife in excitement. "Milan? When? Tomorrow?"

"Not so soon. I want to make quite sure that we make the painting more secure for the journey than we did the last time we left Florence."

The young man frowned, averting his eyes from the portrait. "Need we take it this time?"

"Giacomo, you know very well that wherever I go, she goes. I always need to add to my work on her. You know I never consider her as finished."

"You seldom finish anything. You pursue a hundred different ideas in the course of one afternoon. It's a wonder your head doesn't burst. Painter, draughtsman, engineer, inventor of God only knows what devilish devices...you'll have the Church down on you one day."

The man gave a sardonic smile. "Oh Giacomo, if they only knew one thousandth part of what lives in my head, they would have condemned me to the stake long ago. An ignominious end to poor Leonardo!"

Giacomo shuddered. "Here, have bread and fruit. What would happen to you if I were not here to feed you and at least try to keep you clean?"

"I would be free to work all day uninterrupted." Leonardo smiled at the youth. "And I would probably live like a pig in a sty. The servants would not know how to look after me as you do."

"But you haven't worked all day," Giacomo pointed out reasonably.

"Haven't I? I beg to differ, Master Salai."

"You have merely sat and looked at the Lady Lisa."

"Of course. That looking, as you so ignorantly call it, is the deepest and most significant part of my work."

Giacomo stopped eating and looked worried. "I found something yesterday," he said in more subdued tones. "I happened to glance at your notes in passing and..."

"You touched nothing?" Leonardo gave the young man a sharp look. "You swear?"

"I touched nothing. I merely saw a few words – a phrase – which astonished me."

Leonardo waited, taking a deep draught of wine and wondering what the boy had seen, noting his sudden nervousness.

"I didn't read on. I just saw five words – 'The sun does not move'. That's all."

Leonardo looked at Giacomo with half-closed eyes. "And that worries you?"

"It frightens me. How does the sun not move? All men know it circles the earth ceaselessly. How can you speak against nature like that?"

Leonardo spoke lightly, although he had gone a little paler. "I have strange fancies sometimes, Giacomo. You know that. I trust you not to reveal them to others."

"Never!"

Leonardo pushed the basket of fruit from him and sat back with a deep sigh. "I am so alone, Giacomo."

"Alone? When I am here constantly?"

"You don't understand. It is not that kind of loneliness. I do deeply appreciate your presence here. When you first came here as my servant I knew you would soon be my companion. And now you are also my pupil and will one day be a painter – when I no longer am obliged to retouch your work with my own brush. No, my loneliness lies in my knowledge."

Leonardo leaned forward and helped himself to more wine. "There are secrets of life, Giacomo, which I can share with nobody, not even with you. I have insights which astound even myself. I seem to be acquiring awesome knowledge of the natural laws of existence, simply by plunging deep into my own consciousness. There I perceive things which I can share with no man, If I told the world what I have discovered about itself, the world would destroy me. What if I told you that one day man will fly higher than the birds?"

"What?"

"And sail beneath the sea in enclosed ships of metal? They will see the wreckages of ancient vessels and the bones of drowned sailors."

Giacomo stared in astonished horror. "This is not possible!"

"Everything is possible if the laws of nature are fully understood. Don't you see, Giacomo, that man invents nothing unless he follows nature. We do not conquer nature, we obey it. The more we discover about it, the more we can invent."

"Now you are really making me afraid. This is ungodly! The birds have the air, the fish have the sea, we have the dry land."

"Don't look so frightened, boy. I shall take the greatest care that Mother Church will never have knowledge of what has been revealed to me. But I need to record my knowledge where nobody would dream of looking for it, even if all my works have been destroyed... I am putting it where I can see it looking back at me. Look at the Mona Lisa, Giacomo."

Giacomo turned to the painting. "You have hidden writings somewhere behind the portrait?"

"Nothing so crude. Look at the lady's face. Is she not trying to tell you something? Look at her eyes, that knowing smile. *I am painting my knowledge into her face!*"

"I don't understand. The portrait does not change from day to day."

"Oh, but it does. Any new awareness I am vouchsafed is laid up there as in a treasure chest. Sometimes as an almost invisible smear of misty light along a cheek, a speck of a twinkle in one of the eyes, a subtle and unnoticeable shadow on the side of the forehead – endless secrets deposited with a butterfly's touch, invisible to the onlooker. I share my thoughts with her, she reflects them back to me. We converse in silence, therefore I am not entirely alone in the realm of the mind. Now you see why she accompanies me on my journeys? I am not finishing the work, I am recording my own thinking. This, Giacomo, is a portrait of myself. I am behind that face, gazing out at the onlooker. When I am dead, come and look at this painting. The eyes you see will be full of my thoughts, my memories, for as long as this work lasts."

Giacomo looked at the painting as a jealous wife looks at a mistress. "But when you are dead, who then could possibly benefit from this? Who will know? Onlookers have said that she is enigmatic, sly, secretive, provocative, but who will have the ability to read your own mind in those eyes?"

Leonardo sighed. "Who indeed? Will there be feet shuffling past her as she hangs upon some future wall? And if so, what will people see? Nothing but a tantalising knowingness. Maybe someone, some day..." He sighed again. "I must sleep, Giacomo. Tomorrow I will send a message to the Duke in Milan to let him know we are setting out soon. He said he would expect me in the spring and it is already April. The sooner it is over the better. I am loneliest of all in the courts of the great."

Leonardo rose and ruffled the young man's hair. "Goodnight, my dear boy," he said, and went to his bedchamber.

Giacomo waited until his master and teacher had gone, then stood before the portrait, looking at the face of the wife of Francesco del Giocondo. He reached for the candelabra and held it to the portrait. The painted mouth seemed to smile mockingly as he searched the face for signs of recent addition, but he could detect nothing. The flickering candlelight caused the lips to appear to move. He went to a cluttered table beside a window, searched amongst books, drawings and various small objects until he found the artist's spyglass. This he took back to the portrait, held up the candelabra and peered closely. He felt slightly dizzy as he bent forward, putting the spyglass close to the small mouth with it upturned corners. He moved the glass further away with the effect of the face seeming slightly fuller, the expression more lighthearted as though something had amused the sitter. The mouth was the most changed as the face gradually grew bigger when Giacomo moved the glass further away. Then it seemed to him that the lips parted very slightly and to his horror he thought he saw a shadowed row of little teeth.

Gasping, Giacomo stepped back, bruising his hip against the table. Staring at the portrait, he saw that the mouth was, as usual, firmly closed.

"Too much wine at supper," he muttered. Without a further glance towards the easel he hurried from the room with the candelabra and went to bed, leaving the servants to clear the table of the remains of the meal.

Giacomo was restless all that night and suffered bad dreams until dawn, whilst the lady Giaconda smiled her secret smile alone, a moonbeam from an unshuttered window reflecting as a gleam from her eyes.

Tidal Wave

He hesitated with his hand on the doorknob, fighting against his usual reluctance to walk into a lecture room pulsating with the arrogance of cocksure youth. "*Please don't let George Beckley be there today,*" he prayed, "*and if he is, give him sudden laryngitis and give me a break.*"

Taking a deep breath he pushed open the door and entered the room. All eyes turned towards him as the buzz of conversation stopped.

"Morning, Professor," said several of the students politely.

Professor Alan Higgins, known on the campus as Piggy short for Pygmalion, nodded briefly as he made his way to the lecturer's table. He put a sheaf of papers down on the table and looked around the room. George Beckley was not there.

Alan Higgins had a problem. All his life he had suffered from what he secretly called 'open guts', which colourful appellation accurately described a condition which caused him the utmost distress. It meant that he had no defence whatsoever from feeling under attack when he was merely in the presence of one or more persons. Other people's inward negativity – stress, anger, fear – surged into him without a work being spoken and cramped painfully around his solar plexus, so that whenever he saw anyone approaching he would cautiously place a hand over his stomach. Upon entering a crowded room, he would immediately feel bombarded by resonances from other people's inwardness, resulting in a catastrophic depletion of his own energies.

A result of the 'open guts' syndrome was that the emotionally needy kind of person would subconsciously recognise, in Alan, his involuntary openness and be drawn to him like a pin to a magnet. The needy one would, without being aware of it, suck out his vitality, feed upon it, and then go away strengthened and cheerful, thinking how much better he or she always felt after talking with that nice Professor Higgins. Alan on the other hand would be left physically exhausted and emotionally depleted. He called such people 'feeders' and if he could not avoid them he would desperately try to close his inward door to shut out the invasion, but to no avail, being a man of natural compassion.

George Beckley was his *bete noire*. George was arrogant, intelligent, and had the assurance and cruelty which sometimes went with those attributes. He was quick to recognise weaknesses in others and would seek these out for amusement. Handsome, wealthy and confident, he had seen a vulnerability in Alan from the start of the semester and knew that he could get some fun out of him without trying too hard. He considered the game won when he saw the familiar hunted look in his victim's eyes. But that day George was not there.

Alan went over to the visual aid stand in a calmer state than usual. He exposed the first flip sheet and picked up a black marker pen.

"Alright, let's start with putting down two headings side by side. Pre-Cambrian on the left, Cambrian on the right. Nowadays the great Cambrian so-called explosion is not looked at in quite the same way..."

Suddenly there was a loud and uninhibited yawn. At the same time a dark tousled head reared up from the back of the room where George had been asleep, lying along several chairs. Alan turned from the visual aid stand and stared at George, who was rubbing his eyes and yawning again.

"You *are* with us then, George?" said Alan, causing the other students to giggle.

"Sorry. Had a busy night."

"So let's have a busy morning, shall we?" Alan turned back to the stand feeling that he had neatly scored a point and for the rest of the lecture felt unusually in control, whilst George's stunningly beautiful girlfriend Fiona gave the puffy-eyed youth scornful glances.

Fiona and George had met at the beginning of the semester, and being the most physically attractive of the whole intake of students, each had decided to capture the other before anyone else had a chance. The romance had flamed into a dazzling and rather public affair. Girls envied Fiona and boys envied George and the couple were the centre of attention. But...last night George had been indiscreet with someone else and Fiona was making plans for the future, which did not include George.

***

A few weeks later, Alan was in his study working with his computer when there was a knock at his door.

"Come in!"

Alan continued to work as the intruder – for so Alan's immediate feelings defined him – came into the room.

"Do sit down," said Alan courteously without looking up. He tapped a few more keys, then closed the computer and looked at his visitor.

"Oh, hallo Ackroyd," said Alan, surprised to see the lecturer in Celtic Studies sitting in his armchair. It was the chair everybody made for if they needed comfort or advice, secure in the knowledge that it would be given. Alan placed a protective hand over his stomach in readiness.

"Sorry to bother you, Higgins. I need someone to talk to."

"OK," said Alan, resigned. "Fancy a dram?"

"I don't really like whisky."

"Sherry then?"

"Yes. Thanks."

When they were settled with drinks, Alan cautiously scanned the other, a thin balding man who looked pale and worried.

"So – you wanted to talk. Nothing wrong, I hope?"

"Yes, actually. Daphne's left me."

Alan drew a deep breath and let it out slowly, his hand moving again towards his stomach. He knew from experience that his visitor would go away comforted but leave himself exhausted. It did not bode well for the rest of the day.

"Right then. You'd better tell me about it."

***

The following day Alan had a visit from George. Surprised, he invited him in to his study and indicated the inevitable armchair. George sat down heavily, put his head in his hands and groaned.

"What's wrong, George?"

"Oh God, it's awful! I've got someone pregnant."

"Fiona?"

"No," said George, looking up. The handsome face was haggard. "We've split up. It's a girl I met in a pub a few weeks ago. It was only once – just once! I can't believe it!"

"Yes," mused Alan. "I rather think I know when that was."

"So what do I do now?"

"George, I'm sorry about your trouble, but why did you come to me?"

Alan knew very well why George had chosen him. George knew intuitively that Alan was incapable of repulsing him.

"Because nobody else here seemed right somehow. You're different... kind of more human. I couldn't see myself telling anyone else. What am I going to do?"

"You're sure it's yours?"

George nodded miserably. "It was her first time. She didn't tell me that. What shall I do?" He gazed up hopefully, as though Alan were the Delphic Oracle.

"You keep asking me that, George. Frankly I am ill-equipped to advise you on these matters. You could go to the Welfare Office in the West Block. They deal with all kinds of issues."

"This isn't an issue, it's a tragedy. My Dad will kill me."

"Whyever didn't you use protection?"

"It wasn't meant to happen. I'd had a bit too much to drink and things suddenly got out of hand."

"Yes, but..."

"It happens!"

The conversation continued in this vein until Alan felt weak with fatigue. By the time his visitor left, he had started a migraine and felt very sick, without knowing that George had gone away with a lighter heart, having fed upon Alan's emotional energies and metaphorically grown fat. His troubles were still upon him but he felt stronger, thinking *Old Piggy is really quite a nice guy*.

***

The migraine vomiting went on until one o'clock in the morning. Alan lay back exhausted after the final bout and thought with despair about his situation. *It's as if other people stick a straw into my guts and suck out my strength – and they're only talking, for God's sake!* He thought. *Why does this happen to me? How can I protect myself? These suckers, these feeders, how do they do it? Why do I let them?*

Then it happened. A wave of anger so fierce that it actually shook him began to boil up inside. It coursed like molten lava, first upwards through his chest and throat, actually swelling his neck and then fizzing through his brain, then down his arms and tingling into his fingertips, and finally bursting through his thighs and down to his toes. It was as though a lifetime's habit of self-repression had broken its banks and was flowing freely for the first time, leaving him gasping. He lay quietly for a few moments examining his feelings, then decided that he felt liberated.

"That's it!" he muttered aloud. *No more! Nobody will ever do that to me again. I can still be helpful, but they won't be able to get inside me. My guts belong to me. I'm locking my inner door.*

On this thought he drifted into the deepest sleep he had ever known, and by morning a profound change had taken place. He woke up ravenously hungry and cooked a large fried breakfast, something he had not done for years. Outwardly he was the same man, but inwardly he was experiencing a sense of peace and security. He almost laughed aloud as he printed out some notes from his computer, and as he put them into a file there came a knock at the door.

"Come in!"

The door opened and the beautiful Fiona came in.

"Fiona – this is a surprise. What can I do for you this lovely morning?" He gave her an assured smile, relaxed and confident, and Fiona looked at him with curiosity. This was not the Professor Higgins she knew. Where was the usual anxious, strained expression?

"Sit down, Fiona. We have..." he looked at his wristwatch, "...exactly ten minutes before today's lecture. You seem troubled."

Fiona sank into the armchair and gazed up at Alan. "I'm pregnant. I don't know what to do."

"Good heavens, it must be catching!"

"What? Well, if you're not going to take it seriously..."

"I take it very seriously. It's just that someone else has been to me recently with a similar problem."

"Who?"

"You mustn't ask me to betray confidence."

"Oh. Right. I haven't told George yet. The trouble is – we've split up."

"Oh dear. Quite a muddle." Alan pondered the dilemma, thinking of George's own problem. He was feeling unusually detached and uninvolved, physically restful and mentally alert.

"Well now, my dear," Alan said kindly, "let me suggest one course of action to you as a first step. Go to our Welfare Office for some practical advice of the sort that I am incapable of giving you, then tell George. He has a right to be involved in any decision."

Fiona twisted her handkerchief in nervous fingers for a moment, then nodded.

"But for the moment," continued Alan with an encouraging smile, giving Fiona a fleeting sense of being supported, "we both have a lecture to attend. Shall we go? I'll make palaeontologists of the lot of you if it's the last thing I do."

Fiona was only too willing to wrench her attention away from her terrifying situation, and she trotted beside Alan, thinking what a nice old trout he really was. She had no desire whatsoever to be a mother, only to be a student tackling the most fascinating subject in the world. *Damn George!* She thought resentfully. *They treat us like coffee-vending machines then decide they don't want the coffee.*

For Alan the rest of the day was spent in feelings of wonder, almost awe. He was mentally alert and physically energetic in a way he had never known. It was as if something had washed away his habitual feelings of fear and anxiety, leaving him in control of his own life. Even going into a crowded room caused him no discomfort. If the negative emotions of others were silently bombarding him, they found no foothold and bounced back to their originators. Who knows what discomfort the 'feeders' might be experiencing as their own chickens came home to roost? Alan's inner door was well and truly closed against intrusion. Professor Higgins was completely himself for the first time in his life.

A Pot Of Earl Grey

"Look, here he comes again," said the café waitress.

"Let him, he isn't harming anyone," replied the proprietor.

Into the café came an elderly man with a dignified bearing, clad in incongruous clothes. His shoes were sturdy brown brogues which had seen better days and could have been worn by an intrepid walker of the Pennine Way. He wore shiny blue jeans frayed around the ankles, a prehistoric Harris tweed jacket with leather elbow patches, and the whole outfit was topped by a black baseball cap. He paused in the entrance and scanned the other customers, then made for an empty table in the bow window.

The waitress approached the table, not bothering to take her notepad and pencil from her pocket. "Afternoon, Mr Bellingham. Your usual?"

The man tipped his cap backwards, revealing a tumble of spiky white hair and grinned up at her. "Thank you, dear girl. Pot of Earl Grey and a cream slice. No need to diet at my age." His voice was bluff and genial, just hovering on the edge of hoarseness. A Father Christmas voice, thought the waitress.

The café began to fill up with afternoon tea customers. Mr Bellingham scrutinised them as he ate his cream slice with surprisingly delicacy for a large man with thick stubby fingers.

Eventually he was approached by a middle-aged woman with a heavy shopping bag. "Anyone sitting here?" she asked in a tired voice.

Mr Bellingham spread his hands wide. "Nobody – unless it's the Invisible Man. Sit here by all means, dear lady."

The woman gave him a cautious glance but sat down anyway. She dumped her shopping bag on the seat next to her and looked round for the waitress. Mr Bellingham kept his eyes down and began to pour a cup of black Earl Grey from his teapot, giving the woman the merest flick of a covert glance.

"Good afternoon, madam." The waitress stood with pad and pencil poised. "What can I get for you?"

"A cup of tea and one round of buttered toast, please."

"White or brown toast?"

"White, please."

The waitress went back to the service area and placed the order.

"Has he started yet?" muttered the proprietor.

Knowing what he meant, the waitress shook her head. "Not yet. He's still working out his opening gambit. Keeps looking at her under his eyelids though."

"Doesn't know what she's in for."

The waitress brought tea and toast for the woman, then busied herself clearing and wiping the next table, albeit quite slowly. Mr Bellingham sipped his tea, gazing thoughtfully out of the window.

The woman noticed that Mr Bellingham was drinking black tea. "Oh, here!" she exclaimed, pushing her own miniature carton of milk towards him. "Do have mine. I never touch milk. I always bring my own coffee whitener. It's quite nice in tea."

Mr Bellingham beamed. "That is so kind, dear lady. But your kindness is in vain, I'm afraid. A pot of Earl Grey taken black and I'm more than happy."

The woman gave an embarrassed little smile and drew a small plastic bottle from her handbag. It looked like an aspirin container but was filled with a white powder.

Mr Bellingham glanced at the bottle. "Looks like a heroin fix to me. Main-liner, are you?"

The woman looked serious. "I'm afraid I can't joke about such things," she murmured. "I have a niece in hospital with an overdose. I've just been to see her."

Mr Bellingham was mortified. "My dear lady, do forgive my clumsiness. Of all people I should never take the subject lightly. After all, I did end up in a Far Eastern jail because of drugs."

The woman's eyes widened. "You were an addict?"

"Oh no, no! Don't get me wrong. I was at the time an undercover agent trying to bring a notorious gang of dealers to justice."

The woman's eyes were riveted on Mr Bellingham. "So how did *you* end up in jail and not them?"

Mr Bellingham tapped the side of his nose knowingly. "Oh, you have no idea how resourceful these desperate people are. I was framed. They planted drugs on me, then denounced me to the hotel manager. The drugs were found in my luggage. I didn't have a leg to stand on and the rest is history. It's the oldest trick in the book and I fell for it." He poured more tea and gazed out of the window, sure of the other's attention.

"How absolutely awful!" The woman's eyes were wide with sympathy. "How on earth did you cope?"

"With difficulty. The jail was full of low-lifers – druggies going through cold turkey, thieves, con men, all crowded together. Dante's Inferno!"

The woman bit into her toast, never taking her eyes from the man's face. After a pause she said, "How on earth did you get away from all that?"

"I managed to get a message to the local consul. Had a hell of a job convincing him, though. The sods had stripped me of all my credentials. I could have been any low trickster. Never got my luggage back either. They'd probably sold it by then."

The woman, innocent of the ways of the world, listened in awe. "You could have been a character in a Graham Greene novel," she breathed.

"Nothing so glamorous, I assure you."

The waitress was back at the service counter.

"What's it all about today then?" asked the proprietor with a sideways glance towards Mr Bellingham.

"It isn't half colourful! He's been in prison somewhere in the Far East, mistaken for a drug dealer, when all the time he was an undercover agent trying to catch a gang of real dealers."

"Oh my God, whatever next? He was a test pilot yesterday. Did she buy it?"

"Hook, line and sinker. Look out, the lady's coming over to pay her bill. She's had more than her money's worth today."

Mr Bellingham had risen politely to his feet when his listener had said goodbye and was finishing his tea when a pale young man dressed in a black sweater and black jeans came and sat at his table. After ordering an orange juice and a pink iced cup cake, he took a sheaf of typed papers from his pocket and began to study it with knitted brows. Mr Bellingham, adept at upside-down reading, smiled to himself and took a deep breath. "There is a tide in the affairs of men," he whispered, "which taken at the flood, leads on to fortune…"

The pale young man looked up, startled. "What?"

"That's Julius Caesar, I presume?"

"No, actually," the young man said tartly. "It's the script of a play called On Monday Next. It just happens to have a quotation in it from Julius Caesar, that's all."

"Pardon me, my mistake. You see, I once played Brutus in Julius Caesar in a small theatre off Broadway. Brought back memories."

The young man put down his papers and stared at Mr Bellingham with a tinge of interest. "You're an actor?"

"Oh, long retired. Dodgy health, you understand. But I've had a fantastic time of it – played with most of the greats."

The waitress had heard most of the conversation as she placed the cake and orange juice before the young man. She then set about cleaning debris from nearby tables.

"So what's it like playing Broadway, then? I've never been to America."

"You have to have the hide of a rhinoceros. If the Yankee critics don't like your play on the first night, you're finished. They call them the Broadway Butchers, you know. Even Larry Olivier was in a play there which flopped on the first night. Terrible business."

The young man had relaxed a little. "I'm sure I should know your face but I can't quite place you. Have you been in plays on television?"

"Oh no! I'm strictly a theatre man. Oh, I've had plenty of offers but I need a live audience. Then health problems came along and I retired. Agent still keeps in touch sometimes. Had an offer last week for a radio play. Turned it down, of course. Have you got an agent?"

The young man coughed behind his hand in some embarrassment. "Er – no. Strictly amateur. But I'm going to put in for RADA."

"Good for you, laddie! The race goes to those who run and all that. It's a great life if you can stick at it. Just remember – never let the sods get you down."

"Which sods?"

"The people who won't give you a chance – also the envious ones. They'll stab you in the back with the sweetest of smiles. Having said that, the business is full of the most wonderful people. Find out who they are and you'll never lack true friends."

The waitress put her tray of used crockery on the counter as the proprietor came towards her.

"What's the next tale, then?"

"He's an ex-actor. Played on Broadway. Retired because of his health. Turned down an offer to be in a radio play last week. I can't keep up with him."

When the young aspiring actor had gone, buoyed up with resolution about his future, a woman with a little girl of about eight entered the café. She looked around for a table, then came over to where Mr Bellingham sat.

"Mind if we sit here?" asked the mother.

"Not at all, ma'am. Plenty of room."

The newcomers settled themselves at the table. The child gave Mr Bellingham a look of pure hatred, not wishing to share her mother with anyone else. She was clutching a book close against her chest with a fierce possessiveness.

"Put the book down, Sarah," said the mother.

Reluctantly the child placed the book on the table but kept a forefinger on it. Mr Bellingham read the upside title and said heartily, "Ah! Harry Potter, no less."

Sarah looked at him stonily but said nothing.

"Yes, we've just been queuing up for the latest one," said the mother. "The queue stretched right down the street – I couldn't believe it!"

"I'm not surprised. It's a literary phenomenon. And what does the little lady think of Master Harry Potter then?"

"Answer the gentleman, Sarah," prompted her mother.

"S'alright." Sarah kept her eyes on the book.

"Alright!" The mother laughed. "She's crazy about the books – they all are."

The waitress was hovering with notepad ready.

"Lemonade with a straw and fudge cake for her, please. Tea and buttered scone for me."

Mr Bellingham was looking thoughtfully at the book. "The idea of magic… always such a lure for children," he murmured. "Always has been, always will be."

"You're right there."

"It's all around us, of course."

"Oh yes. Alice In Wonderland, fairy tales…"

"No. I mean magic itself."

Sarah's attention was captured. The lure had been set at just the right moment and the hard gaze softened to cautious interest.

"Our adult perceptions are limited, you know. Very young kids have cognitions on a level we know nothing about. As they grow older they lose it, just as we lost it."

The child was looking intently at Mr Bellingham, who avoided her gaze. Something inside her was bursting to express itself but she had no words to articulate her feelings. Instead she placed the palm of her hand on the book. Mr Bellingham understood and turned his head to look closely at her. "That's why children need books like Harry Potter, The Wizard Of Earthsea, Puck Of Pook's Hill, etc. Isn't that right?" he said, looking at Sarah with a solemn expression. Sarah nodded, and the mother gave her a puzzled and rather irritated look.

The waitress came with a tray which she unloaded. "Orange juice, fudge cake, tea, buttered scone. Anything else, madam?"

"No thanks, that's fine. Now don't get anything sticky on that nice new book, Sarah."

Mr Bellingham sensed the child's sudden withdrawal as the mother's words clashed with the will-o'-the-wisp driftings of her own mind, making her attend closely to orange juice and cake for protection.

Mr Bellingham sighed. "How sad that we can't see the magic all around us any more."

Sarah just managed to stop herself saying "I can!"

"It's everywhere," continued Mr Bellingham. "In the sun, the moon, the stars. In the rainbow, the flowers, the forests, the icebergs. Everything's made of nature's magic. Didn't the Bard himself say that we are such stuff as dreams are made of?"

Sarah was now looking at him with such understanding that Mr Bellingham caught his breath.

The mother was stony-faced. "Eat up, Sarah. We have a train to catch."

The child did not look at the mother. She kept her gaze downwards to hide resentment, momentarily akin to hatred.

"Well?" said the proprietor to the waitress. "So what's the new story then?"

"Don't know. I've been busy the other side of the room. We've missed out on that one."

"I think the best one was when he nearly got eaten by a shark," reminisced the proprietor.

"Oh no, I liked the one where he was climbing a mountain, fell down a ravine and said he could look up and see the stars in broad daylight. Oh look, that mother and little girl are coming to pay."

Sarah paused at the exit, turned and looked back at Mr Bellingham. She clutched her book against her chest with one hand and with the other she wiggled her fingers at Mr Bellingham in farewell. He waved back, and for a moment they exchanged a long look.

"Sarah! For goodness sake come on!"

Five minutes later a Jamaican student was being regaled with a story of how Mr Bellingham had subdued a wild lion in Africa, simply by using the power of the human eye. "Look any domestic pussycat in the eye for long enough and it will grow uneasy," explained Mr Bellingham. "You see, it doesn't know what you are going to do. And what's a lion but a big cat?"

The student was polite but unimpressed. Mr Bellingham decided to re-order and signalled to the waitress. "Another pot of the fragrant black stuff, dear girl!"

The proprietor glanced at the student. "Young chap doesn't seem too impressed."

"Can't win 'em all, can he? Now he wants another…"

"…pot of Earl Grey. And look, here comes another victim taking the young chap's place. It's marvellous what tales can come out of a teapot."

Epona's Well

"Looking for a trip out, Mrs Drew?" The hotel manager peered over Joan's shoulder at the display of leaflets in the foyer. "I can recommend that river trip. There's the cathedral, of course. Lots of our visitors go there. There's the zoo, plenty of country walks, Pony's Well..."

"Pony's Well?" said Joan, trying not to feel irritated by the man's eagerness. "What's that?"

"An ancient well in a forest glade, about two miles away. Here, take the leaflet, there's a little map on the back."

Donald Drew arrived and looked enquiringly at the leaflet in his wife's hand.

"It's a trip to an old well," she said. "Sounds interesting."

"It's worth a visit," put in the manager. His enthusiasm was invasive and Joan stepped back a little. "There's a café and a small museum too – quite enough to fill a morning."

"What kind of museum?" asked Donald.

"It's all to do with things found in and around the well throughout the ages. Might I suggest you visit the museum first? It would give more interest when you see the well."

"Let's take a look at some of the other leaflets too," said Donald, making a selection and not wanting to be told how to spend his holiday. "We can decide later." Nevertheless it was the well they decided upon.

They had to drive through a wooded area before they came to a clear space, where they saw a café named Pony's Place next to a small building which they rightly guessed was the museum. As they parked and climbed out of the car, Donald gave a deep groan.

"Now what?"

"Just look at that!"

Joan's gaze followed his pointing finger. "Oh. Yes. I see what you mean."

She was looking at a signpost in the shape of a huge cartoon hand indicating a pathway into the adjacent wood. It bore the legend

'Pony's Well' and beneath this were the words: 'See the Fairy Well in the Druids' Grotto and Make a Wish as you Throw a Coin'. Then in smaller letters it read: 'All proceeds to the upkeep of the Well and Museum'.

"Come on," said Donald, turning back to the car. "Let's go to the cathedral. We can get lunch in the refectory there."

"Oh, don't let's just run off now we're here. Anyway I need a cup of coffee. Let's go to the café first and then see how we feel."

"OK, but don't get too excited. This is the usual tourist trap."

In the café they seated themselves at a table where Joan picked up a shiny plastic menu headed by a profile of a black rearing pony in one corner.

"Mm... I've changed my mind about coffee. They've got hot chocolate with cream. How about you?"

"Coffee. Look, it seems we have to go over there and pick up a tray. You stay here, I'll go. Anything to eat?"

"No thanks. I'll wait for the cathedral refectory at lunch time."

"Oh good, we are going then," said Donald with feeling. "The leaflet says they've got some interesting stained glass. Beats all this rubbish." He stalked away towards the display of food and drinks, feeling more cheerful.

***

Donald declined to go to the museum first simply because the hotel manager had suggested that they should. They made their way along the path into the wooded area, until it began to slope slightly downwards, where the trees and bushes grew thicker and the filtering daylight became dimmer. They came to a fork in the path, where Donald gave a derisive snort and pointed to a Walt Disney garden gnome on the ground, who was indicating the path to the left with a long gnarled finger.

"Ridiculous!" said Joan. "Now they've lost all credibility. Do you want to go on?"

Donald shrugged. "Might as well, if only to see how twee they can get. There's probably a plastic bucket on a wind-up rope."

There wasn't. The first thing they became aware of was the fact that several bushes around the well were festooned with pieces of cloth, coloured ribbons and lengths of bright wool, with occasional twists of silver or gold foil. One piece of red ribbon had been so teased by constant movement that it had become like red cobweb.

"We seem to be alone," remarked Donald, looking around as they approached the well.

"No bucket. No rope."

"And no water," added Donald, peering down.

"I thought all wells had water."

"Not if their underground springs have dried up. It looks as if this one dried up centuries ago."

"But then," objected Joan, "it isn't a real well any more, is it? It's a con. Look at the brickwork round the rim. That's modern."

Donald, in a contrary mood, said, "No, wait. Look further down. It's all much older down there. They probably had to reinforce the rim for safety reasons. See how far down it goes? A fall down there would kill anyone." A glint from the darkness below caught his eye. "There's money down there. Any coins in your purse?"

Joan fumbled in her purse and pulled out two ten pence pieces. "That's all the loose change I've got."

"Chuck it in, then. Make a wish. Might as well go the whole hog."

Joan threw the money into the darkness and wished. As she did so the sunlight disappeared and a cold little breeze moved amongst the bushes.

Joan shivered. "Let's go and look at the museum. This doesn't seem much of a Druids' Grotto to me."

"Oh, that's just their fancy way of making money. I wonder how they get down there to collect it?"

"Easy. Down that ladder."

Donald looked and saw an iron ladder clamped to the inside wall, blending in so well that in the dimness it was scarcely noticeable.

"Wouldn't like that job myself," said Donald as they walked away.

***

The museum turned out to be more interesting. There were several glass exhibition cases featuring ancient offerings found in the well. There were rings, buckles, dress pins, any amount of coins from different periods of history, including Roman. Around the walls there were large blown-up photographs, the oldest ones in black and white or sepia, depicting former excavations. In one of these a man stood proudly beside what looked like a carved relief in stone, which leaned crookedly against his legs as he smiled at the camera through a drooping moustache.

"I can understand people throwing coins, it's an old custom," remarked Joan, "but why hang ribbons and strips of cloth on bushes?"

"An equally old custom in many parts of the British Isles, madam," said a voice behind them.

They turned and saw a small, balding man wearing thick spectacles, who smiled apologetically. "Do excuse me for butting in, but I'm the curator and it's my habit to stroll about listening to the comments of visitors. And, of course, to answer any questions."

"Oh good," said Joan, brightening. "About these ribbons, then?"

"Possibly an offering for the healing of illnesses, or maybe the granting of wishes. Healing is the most probable. Did you notice that there were some thorn bushes around the well? In the old days it was quite a common practice to plant groves of these bushes around sacred wells. Thorns may have been dropped into healing wells because they represented the pains of sickness or injury. From that would have developed the habit of throwing in pins and nails. Over there is an exhibit displaying bent pins and rusty nails found at deep levels of the well. Deeper still they found nails from Roman sandals, as well as Roman coins."

"So this well must have been here before the Roman invasion?" put in Donald.

"Well before – no pun intended," smiled the curator, pleased to be able to discuss his interests. "The most fascinating find was in 1920 when they dug up a stone bas-relief of a Celtic deity. There are others in existence, but this one is ours. There she is, in that photograph on the wall beside her proud discoverer."

"Maybe she's the goddess of the well, then?" said Joan. "A kind of water-nymph?"

Donald had put on his reading glasses and was peering at the photograph. "Good heavens," he muttered. "What in the world is she doing here? You say she was excavated here?"

The curator beamed. "Oh yes. Just a few feet from the well, in fact. It is highly likely that it depicts the original deity of the well. Her name is…"

"Europa!" said Donald, taking off his glasses.

The curator looked puzzled. "Oh no, my dear sir. You are confusing two admittedly rather similar names."

"But I've seen her before."

"Oh? Where?"

"Lullingstone."

"But that's a Roman Villa. There's nothing of this nature there. Epona is of Celtic origin."

Donald put his glasses on again and looked closely at the photograph. "If this isn't a Celtic version of Europa and the Bull then I don't know what to make of all these amazingly coincidental features. A young woman sitting side-saddle on the back of a large four-footed animal. Could be a horse, or possibly a bull. She has short curly hair, quite modern-looking. She wears a short skirt and one knee is slightly raised. She holds in each hand the end of some sort of large cloth which floats over her head in an arc, like a rainbow. Her left hand has to be imagined as it is obscured by the head of the animal. She wears some kind of bracelet on her right wrist. When was the last time you visited Lullingstone?"

"I don't quite remember – some time ago – but…"

"Do you remember seeing a mosaic of Europa and the Bull?"

"Of course. It's famous."

"Well, every detail I have just described in your photograph is exactly echoed in the Europa mosaic."

The curator took off his spectacles and polished them with a pristine handkerchief taken from his breast pocket. He blinked downwards as he polished vigorously. "I really feel I can't pronounce on this, sir." He replaced his spectacles. "However, let me tell you something about Epona. She is known at the Great Mare Goddess. That animal on which she is seated is in fact a horse. During the Roman period she was enthusiastically taken up by the Romans, especially the cavalry. Their horses were of primary importance to them, and Epona was a horse goddess. Shrines to Epona appeared all over Europe, including a few in Britain. She was also associated with water and with healing. Our well here is almost certainly a healing well, and it seems pretty conclusive that Epona was its presiding deity. We not only found the bas-relief near the well, but also the remains of an ancient shrine. There was not enough of the shrine left for us to reconstruct it. After the Romans left it is likely that local people plundered the shrine to build walls or homes. It happened everywhere when the Romans withdrew and everything was up for grabs. It was a miracle they didn't find the carving or it would have been used as a hearthstone or a sharpening stone. So weren't we lucky?"

"They might have left it alone because they were superstitious," suggested Joan.

The curator turned to her in relief. "Yes, madam, that could well have been the case. Now could I suggest that we go into my office? I have books there on several subjects, including Roman Britain. With any luck we may find a picture of Europa somewhere. Would you like to come with me?"

It was a small stuffy office with a desk, several filing cabinets, and a computer in one corner. At the far end was a bookshelf holding about twenty books.

"Please sit down," said the curator, going to the bookshelf. "Now let me see – oh yes, here we are." He carried a large book to the desk, sat down and turned to the index. "Europa... Europa... yes, Page twenty-one. Yes, yes, here it is – the mosaic in question." He pushed the book towards the others.

Joan looked carefully at the picture before speaking. "Yes, I do see what Donald means. There's the same short curly hair, a bracelet on the right wrist, holding up a cloth like an arch over her head. And she sits side-saddle on the animal and you can't see the left hand because it's behind the animal's head. Short skirt just the same, one knee raised. If it were not for the fact that Epona's animal is a horse and Europa's is a bull, I'd be tempted to think they were the same person. Could a new Celtic deity have been inspired by the Roman legend of Europa and the Bull?"

"Or," put in Donald eagerly, "perhaps some Celtic artist of the Occupation has tried to assimilate Epona to Europa in a more modern version of his own? It reminds me of the Greek occupation of ancient Egypt, when they equated their god of healing, Asklepios, with the more ancient Egyptian healer Imhotep."

The curator pursed his lips. "Both interesting theories, of course, and I do sympathise with your thoughts. Certainly some new Celtic deities did appear during the Roman Occupation, but it is highly unlikely that Epona was one of them."

"But the similarities?" insisted Donald. "They are so exactly alike in all respects. How do you account for that?"

The curator shrugged. He was growing tired. "Coincidence?"

Joan perceived his fatigue and changed the subject. "The name Pony's Well – is that really Epona's Well?"

The curator gave what seemed to Joan a rather condescending smile. "We have managed to work that one out, madam. Even though many centuries have passed, the name, though somewhat distorted, has managed to survive all the changes in local language."

"I'd love to see the carving itself," said Joan. "Is it here somewhere?"

"No, not here. They sent it to a bigger museum in the next town for safe-keeping many years ago."

He saw the disappointment on her face. He felt in his desk drawer and pulled out a leaflet. "Here, take this. The museum isn't far away. It tells you how to get there."

"That's very kind. That settles where we can go tomorrow. Thank you so much for taking the trouble to talk to us."

The curator watched them go with profound relief.

***

Once outside the museum, Joan said, "Do let's go back and see the well again. I now think of it as Epona's Well. Let's go and say goodbye to her."

"It was probably all coincidental, you know," mumbled Donald as they retraced their footsteps.

"What?"

"All that Europa stuff. Wishful thinking on my part."

"Not with all those details matching so precisely, surely. I wish we knew a few Romano-Celtic scholars we could talk to."

"Well, we don't. Here's that ghastly garden gnome again. Left turn!"

When they reached the well the sunlight was again dappling itself around the Druid's Grotto. Joan leaned over the rim of the well and looked down. "I wonder how long ago it dried up?" she said, half to herself. "I wonder how many generations worshipped Epona here? I wonder when she became forgotten?"

"You're doing a hell of a lot of wondering. Are you wearing any hairpins?"

"What?" Joan straightened. "Well, no. I've got a couple in my handbag. Why?"

"Get one out and drop it down the well."

"I've already dropped two coins."

"Indulge me. I've a fancy to make a farewell gesture."

"But why a hairpin?"

"It would seem that generations of droppers-in have been throwing down various kinds of pins for centuries. Go on, just for a lark. You wanted to say goodbye to Epona, didn't you?"

Joan scrabbled her fingers through the contents of her bag and eventually brought out a hairpin. As she made to throw the pin, Donald stopped her.

"Not yet. Make a wish."

"I already made one last time."

"Make another."

Joan stared at him. "Have you been out in the sun too long? OK, here goes then."

The sunlight dimmed and the trees hissed slightly as the breeze strengthened. Joan gave a little shudder.

"A funny thing," said Joan as they began to walk away from the well. "Each time I made a wish it seemed to get cold for a moment. Did you notice?"

"Can't say I did. What did you wish?"

"You're not supposed to ask."

"Oh, go on."

"No."

"OK. Cathedral. Refectory. Stained glass windows. Not necessarily in that order. What did you wish?"

"The same wish I made last time. You're going to keep on, aren't you?"

"Yes."

They argued in this fashion until they reached the car, and all the while a small damp patch was silently spreading at the bottom of the well.

***

They were seated at lunch in the cathedral refectory when Donald renewed his attack. "Oh come on, Joan. You don't really believe all that superstitious stuff about wishes not coming true if you tell, do you?"

"No. Yes. Oh, I don't know. Alright, I'll tell you and if it doesn't come true I shall blame you."

"Fair enough."

"I wished that the old spring that used to feed the well would find its way back. I want it to be a proper well again – Epona's Well."

The damp patch was now a puddle as big as the lid of a jam jar.

"That's great! Even though it will never happen."

"But it might. Some farmer or builder might go digging around in that area and disturb the earth so that underground water has to flow in a different direction. Anything could happen. Water came there once – it could again."

Donald shrugged, then lifted his glass of water. "Here's to Epona's Well. As I drink this water, so new water will flow into the well." He drank deeply. "Now, how about dessert. I fancy ice cream."

In the afternoon they visited the town museum. By the time they stood admiring the bas-relief of the Great Mare Goddess, the well was about one-eighth full of water and rising.

Love Is Blind

Venus was in a cowshed being adored by the herd, their soft eyes radiating love for her. Her fingers were playing with the furry ears of their leader when Cupid came running into the shed, stubbing his chubby foot against the round stone used by the twenty-first century peasants as a doorstep.

"Bugger!" he hissed, bending to rub his foot.

Venus spun round and glared at her son. "What have I told you about using bad language? It's most inappropriate for people in our position."

"We're not exactly *people* are we? So it doesn't really matter, does it?"

"Don't quibble. It's your own fault you fall over everything – always in such a hurry."

Cupid snatched the blindfold from his eyes and held it out, shaking it beneath his mother's nose. "No, it's this damned thing. How do you expect me to see anything wearing this all the time? No wonder I make people fall in love with the wrong partners. Only yesterday I shot an arrow at a soldier and he fell in love with a pig. Now that's what you can call inappropriate. I'm fed up!"

"It's no use complaining," retorted Venus, patting her perfect hair. "It's the way Almight Jupiter ordained things since the beginning of time. We all have to fulfil our various duties, don't we?"

Cupid sat on a straw bale and nursed his foot. "It might interest you to know that I sent a memo to His Heavenly Lordship yesterday, suggesting that I should be allowed to see where I direct my arrows. I should be able to know what I'm doing."

Venus gasped and held onto the wooden rails of the cowpen. "What? You questioned the decree of the Obergruppengod? He'll send you a thunderbolt to blast you to smithereens! You absolute fool!"

"No he won't. I've been doing this job for thousands of years. He needs me."

"Oh yes, like he needs a hole in the head. And just how many arrows have you shot today? I see your quiver's still half full, and it's nearly sunset."

Cupid sniffed. "Fell asleep, didn't I? I'm tired. I think I'm anaemic. Need a holiday."

"Gods don't take holidays, as the world well knows. What would happen to the human race if we went about taking holidays?"

"They don't even know we're still here, Ma. They've got computers now. Sickles are out, they've got combine harvesters. Need I go on?" Cupid stood up and stretched his child-like body. "Look at me! Why the hell did our Divine Overlord give me a baby's body?"

"Because you personify innocence, idiot. You shoot your love-darts without guile. You *have* to look like a baby."

Cupid looked down at himself with disgust. "And look at this stupid loin cloth – it looks like a nappy. I'm, embarrassed. I wouldn't mind the job so much if I could wear jeans and a T-shirt."

"We are what we are, Cupid. If we were to change the world would end."

"No it wouldn't."

"Yes it would. We make everything work, all of us. We make the seasons come on time, the rain fall, the sun and moon and stars do the right thing…"

"Oh yes," sneered Cupid, "while Jupiter snoozes on a cloud safe in the knowledge that his underlings are pulling all the strings for humans."

Venus sighed and turned back to the worshipping cows for another intake of love, knowing that at least the animals knew what was what. "Get back to work, Cupid, and don't come home until your quiver is empty," she said dreamily.

Cupid turned on his fat little heel and stomped towards the shed door, muttering under his breath.

"Wait!"

Cupid stopped.

"You haven't put your blindfold on."

With a groan, Cupid bound the blindfold around his head and continued to the door, where he stubbed his foot again. He ran until he thought he was out of earshot, then released a string of colourful expletives, most of which he had picked up in the 'Sixties of the twentieth century'.

"I heard that!"

***

Cupid came to the edge of a wood, where he pulled down his blindfold and looked around. He saw a young man sitting on a fallen tree reading a letter. The man wore a winged hat and sported wings on his heels.

"Hi, Mercury," said Cupid. "Are you coming or going?"

The young man looked up. "Depends on your point of view."

"Don't play damned silly games with me," snapped Cupid. "Are you on your way to Jupiter with my message, or on your way back to me with his reply?"

"On my way back, of course. They don't call me Quicksilver for nothing, you know. Here you are then. I just stopped to read it."

"You read my correspondence? How dare you!"

Cupid snatched the letter and glared at Mercury, who merely shrugged.

"I always read the messages. It relieves the tedium. That one's a bit boring, though. His Divinity goes on and on *ad nauseum* about doing one's celestial duty and all that jazz."

"Yes, I can see that, thank you," said Cupid, scanning the letter. "He doesn't seem to understand that I need to see while I'm working. If I knew what I was doing there wouldn't be half so many divorces. Oh well, that's that I suppose." Cupid tore the letter into little pieces and scattered them over the ground. "I feel like giving up this job."

Mercury was looking thoughtful. "What exactly did His Divinity decree that you should do?"

"Shoot arrows and make people fall in love, of course. I thought everyone knew that – I've been doing it for centuries."

"Yes, but what else? What did he say about the blindfold?"

"That I should wear it at all times when I'm working."

"Right. But he didn't say anything about what kind it should be, did he?"

"I don't follow you."

Mercury grinned. "He didn't specify that you shouldn't wear one with holes in it, did he?"

"No... what do you mean?"

"I'll show you." Mercury took a knife from a bag attached to his belt. "Give me your blindfold."

Delicately, using only the tip of his knife, the Winged Messenger of the Gods cut two small holes in Cupid's blindfold, then handed it back to the cherubic little god.

"There you go. Put it on."

Cupid obeyed, and then gasped. "Yes! Yes, yes, yes! Whyever didn't I think of that?"

"You'll be a bit tunnel-visioned, but at least you *have* vision. Now perhaps you won't be responsible for so many ghastly unsuitable couplings."

Cupid frowned. "But what will happen to the saying amongst humans, 'Love is Blind'?"

"Oh, that'll take care of itself. People will think it means that the lover is blind to the faults of the beloved. Don't worry about it."

"Thanks, Mercury – I owe you one. Got something I can write on?"

"Yes. Why?"

"I'll just scribble a note to Jupiter assuring him of my penitence and everlasting obedience to his divine will, then you can carry it back to him."

Mercury groaned. "Backwards and forwards, here, there and everywhere – it never stops. His Nibs won't let us use e-mails, of course. Must stick to the old ways or the world would fall to pieces." He put a hand into his bag and drew out writing materials. "Here you are then. Make it short, I need to sleep before I set off again. I don't know where Mars gets his energy from. I met him two days ago coming back from starting a fracas between villages in Outer Mongolia – and he's in bad odour with Neptune for starting a battle between two rival pirate ships in the China seas, just when the old boy thought the whole ocean was settling down to a calm period."

"Mars is always looking for a scrap, you'll never change him. Here's my letter then, short and sweet. And thanks for the brainwave, you're a star. I might even begin to enjoy my job now."

***

A few days later Cupid came back to the celestial palace he shared with Venus. He was pale and haggard, his feet dragged, his loin cloth drooped down to his dimpled knees and his quiver was empty of arrows.

"What time do you call this?" demanded Venus. "Where have you been? I've been worried sick!"

Cupid collapsed onto a cloudy floating divan. "I'm finished!" he moaned. "I can't go on."

"Whyever not? Kindly explain yourself."

"I saw them all before I shot my arrows."

"What? Are you telling me you removed your blindfold?"

"No."

"What, then?"

"I'm telling you I saw my victims as plainly as I see you now."

"But you can't see me – you're wearing your blindfold."

Cupid took off the blindfold and poked two fingers through the holes. Venus turned pale.

"Then," continued Cupid, "just as I was beginning to have more fun than I've ever had – I heard this awful voice. It was everywhere and nowhere – sort of inside my head. It told me off something rotten for what I'd done in a most terrifying way. I nearly died of fright!"

"Jupiter!" whispered Venus, staring around in terror.

"That's right, Lady Venus!" roared a voice which shook the whole palace. "That stupid boy forgot that I am omnipresent, omniscient and omnipotent. He will never disobey my decree again! Will you, boy?"

Cupid trembled. "No, Your Divinity," he breathed.

"Lady Venus, you will take better care of that brat from now on, will you not?"

"Yes, Your Divinity," squeaked Venus hastily.

Suddenly the room was normal again. His Divinity had removed his presence from their perception.

Venus turned on Cupid. "You little fool! That could have been the end of both of us! Don't you ever do anything like that again!"

"No, Ma," quavered Cupid.

"And please don't call me Ma – it's so ageing."

Cupid looked pathetic, his face upturned to his eternally beautiful mother as she stood frowning down fiercely upon her errant offspring. He held the mutilated blindfold up so that it dangled sadly from his fat little fingers.

"Please would you make me a new one?"

The Angel And The Spider

At exactly six o'clock, Philip heard his lounge telephone ringing as he put his key into the lock. He sighed impatiently as he let himself into the flat, having been looking forward to a quiet Friday evening after a stressful working week. He flung down his briefcase and picked up the telephone.

"Philip Sheldon!" His tone was terse.

"Oh dear, you sound tense. It's only me, Phil," said his mother.

Philip sighed again. "Yes, mother."

"I'm just ringing to say don't ring me tonight. I'm having a little bridge party and you know how the phone interrupts the game. Just take this as our Friday night call, dear. Alright?"

"OK, ma. Have a good game. Bye!"

Thankfully Philip poured a small whisky and sank into an armchair, breathing 'Deep joy!' which was an expression he remembered his late father using.

Later he finished his whisky and went to have a bath. Before undressing he reached to turn on the taps. Suddenly he became rigid with horror. In the bath stood a huge black spider, menace in every bent leg. Then began the familiar sweating, the shaking, the lurching of the stomach, the rapid breathing. He was trapped in yet another episode of the arachnophobia which had plagued him since early childhood. Hypnosis and other therapies had completely failed, leaving him vulnerable to hysteria at the mere sight of even the smallest of the creatures.

For a full five minutes he stood frozen, loathing the sight of the eight-legged monstrosity. "This is ridiculous!" he muttered at last. "It can't hurt me, it isn't as though it's poisonous. Even if it touched me..." he shuddered at the thought, "...it can't do any harm. Oh shut up, you fool! You know you don't believe a word of that."

He stepped back cautiously. The spider moved slightly, as though giving a little jump with all eight legs, and he froze again. For a moment he wondered if it was capable of getting out of the bath. The thought galvanised him and he bolted from the bathroom, slamming the door behind him.

He collapsed into the armchair and wiped his forehead with shaking fingers. "Why am I like this?" he murmured helplessly, gazing at the window where the twilight was deepening. "If I believed in guardian angels I'd ask for help."

The telephone rang. Listlessly he put out a hand and picked up the receiver. "Philip Sheldon."

"Oh dear, you sound tense. It's only me, Phil," said his mother.

Something began to buzz strangely inside his head.

"I'm just ringing to say don't ring me tonight." The buzzing sensation increased. "I'm having a little bridge party and you know how the phone interrupts the game. Just take this as our Friday night call, dear."

He found himself saying, "OK, ma. Have a good game. Bye."

He replaced the receiver delicately, as though it might explode. *Keep calm*, he thought. "There must be an explanation. Impossible things can't happen. That bloody spider has thrown me into shock."

He leaned back and closed his eyes, feeling the sensation in his head. The buzzing suddenly stopped, replaced by a silence so intense that it felt like a physical pressure.

"Don't worry," he heard a voice say quite distinctly. "This is the only way I can get through to you."

Philip leapt from the chair and looked wildly round the room, clutching a cushion to his chest for comfort.

"Oh, you can't see me," continued the voice. "You see, I've always been with you but you have never called me. Until now, that is. Didn't know you had a guardian angel, did you?" Philip staggered back to his chair and sank down, white-faced. He looked at his empty whisky glass, thinking that he could not possibly be drunk after such a small amount.

"No, you're not drunk," assured the voice. "Not mad either. I'm here to help you, so just go with the flow. Now – you don't like spiders, do you?"

Philip put his hand to his head and looked intently around the room, peering into the furthest corners.

"Don't waste time looking for me," said the voice. "Just answer the question."

"OK – I hate the sods."

"Right. And you don't know why, do you?"

"No."

"Well, I do. I've been with you since before you were born. Something happened a long time ago. You have forgotten all about it."

"Wait a minute. You're just a figment of my imagination, probably brought on by shock. Get out of my head."

"Do you want to lose your fear of spiders?"

"Yes, but..."

"Alright, so let me help. I've waited thirty-two of your years for this. Trust me, I'm for real."

"You don't even talk like an angel."

"So how are angels supposed to talk, then?"

"Well, kind of – biblical, I suppose."

The voice exploded into peals of laughter. "Give me one good reason why an eternal being like myself can't talk in any age. I know how to use the jargon of the thirtieth century. You have no idea of how the language will change. It will be as different as Chaucerian language sounds to you today. So let's get down to business here. Your fear is rooted in your past. We'll go back and face it. I've already started you on that journey by taking you back to six o'clock when your mother rang."

"Oh? I thought I was going mad."

"Now we'll go further. Close your eyes, relax."

Philip, aware that he had nothing to lose, obeyed the voice. Immediately his thoughts jumped back to boarding school.

"Look into the darkness behind your eyelids. Feel how friendly it is. You are thinking about your boyhood, aren't you? School?"

"Yes. Horrible. Don't want to think about it."

"That will do nicely. Now – open your eyes."

Philip opened his eyes in some anxiety. He found that he was lying in an uncomfortable narrow bed in a long room full of similar beds. He knew that he was a small boy wearing pyjamas and that the other beds were occupied by other boys.

"Are you ready, Benson?" whispered a boy in the opposite bed.

"Ready," hissed his neighbour.

"Have you got it?"

"Course I have."

"Come on, then!"

Two small boys rose from their beds, one carrying a small glass jar with a lid. Philip watched them approach his bed with growing apprehension. He knew that something bad was about to happen – something very bad.

"Hallo, Sheldon. Having trouble sleeping?" said one of the boys with a disarming grin.

"That's too bad," said the other boy. "Maybe this will help." He unscrewed the lid of the jar, held the jar upside down over Philip's chest and banged it with his fist. A large spider fell out with a sickening plop onto Philip's chest. He heard himself screaming as the other boys scrambled back to their beds, laughing hysterically.

"Alright, open your eyes," said the voice calmly.

Philip was sweating and shaking. "No more!" he gasped. "I'm not having any more of that. I thought you were going to help me. Go away!"

"I *am* helping you. Bear with me."

"No! Why did you put me through that?"

"I have my reasons. Close your eyes again."

"No!"

"Then unfortunately I shall have to make you do it. Close your eyes."

Philip felt himself unable to keep his eyes open. He felt a soft breeze on his face. Opening his eyes, he found himself lying on his back in a baby's pram beneath a huge sycamore tree at the end of a garden. As he looked upwards, he saw with delight how the leaves were rustling and twinkling in the breeze, revealing glimpses of a vivid blue sky. He gurgled with happiness as he felt himself one with the tree, the leaves, the sky – as though he were part of it.

As he looked with almost unbearable exhilaration – all his unfolding senses at their most intense – something very different happened. Down from the tree, slowly and menacingly, descended a speckled brown spider on an unwinding thread. Exhilaration turned to horror. All his heightened senses latched on to the sight. The creature dropped closer and closer until it landed on the screaming baby's neck, where it began to crawl up towards his jaw.

"Harmless," said a quiet voice. "Completely harmless. Calm and quiet now. Nothing to fear. Look. Here comes mother. She'll simply pick it up and drop it onto the grass. You feel peaceful, at one with everything. That was just a friendly little creature come to say hallo. There it goes, running off through the grass. Now open your eyes."

Philip opened his eyes, feeling strangely tranquil. "What happened?" he asked. "I can't remember."

"No need for you to remember."

"But something has changed. Why don't you explain?"

"I took you back to the time when you were a tiny baby. There was an incident involving a spider which triggered off all your future fears. That incident has been – shall we say manipulated in your memory? Now we can proceed. Close your eyes."

"What – again?" But this time Philip obeyed, relishing the full feeling of tranquillity.

"Right, now open your eyes."

Philip did so. He saw that he was once again lying in his pyjamas in bed in the school dormitory.

"Are you ready, Benson?" whispered the boy in the opposite bed.

"Ready."

"Have you got it?"

"Yes."

"Come on then."

The two boys rose from their beds, one carrying a glass jar with a lid. Philip watched them approach his bed with calm interest. He knew exactly what was about to happen.

"Hallo, Sheldon. Having trouble sleeping?" grinned one of the boys."

"That's too bad," said the other boy. "Maybe this will help."

He began to unscrew the lid. Philip sat up, grabbed the boy's wrist and wrenched the jar away from him. He continued the unscrewing, removed the lid and tipped a large spider inside the boy's pyjama jacket. The boy yelled and danced about, tearing at the jacket.

"That will do nicely," said the voice. "You can open your eyes now."

Philip looked around his lounge, feeling a deep sense of peace and strength.

"Alright," said the voice cheerfully. "That's all. Now we are at the moment when you decided to have a bath. You won't remember a thing about all this. At least, not until you need me again."

"But – all that stuff in the dormitory. It simply didn't happen like that."

"No, of course it didn't. But now the cells in your nervous system remember differently. Arachnophobia is now a thing of the past, as far as they are concerned. They are no longer passing on the fear of spiders to future generations of cells."

"Ever thought of becoming a celestial psychiatrist?"

"Now there's an idea."

Philip sighed. "Well, all I can say is – thank you."

"No need. And now it's bath time. I've held the moment for you. Off you go then, and goodbye. Now forget."

Philip finished his whisky and went to have a bath. Before undressing he bent to turn on the taps. A huge black spider stood in the bath as though defying all comers, hairy legs bent for action. Philip felt strangely calm. He opened the bathroom window, picked up a small towel and dropped it over the spider, imprisoning the creature. He scooped up towel and spider, walked without haste to the window and shook out the towel. He leaned forward and watched the creature land on the windowsill of the bathroom beneath his own, then to his consternation saw it scuttle through the open window.

Hope I haven't given someone a problem, he thought, and then undressed and luxuriated in a steamy bath.

As he was dressing he heard a scream which seemed to come from the flat directly below. As quickly as he could, he left the flat and ran for the lift, still towelling his hair. He rang the bell of the flat immediately below his own. The door opened to reveal a pretty girl in a dressing gown holding a long-handled fluffy duster. She looked pale and frightened.

"Excuse me ringing your bell, but I thought I heard a scream. Are you alright."

"No! Are you afraid of spiders?"

"No." His answer came without hesitation.

"Oh, thank God! Could you possibly help me?"

She ushered him into the flat and took him through to the bathroom. "Look! A monster!"

Philip regarded the spider coolly. "Mm. Quite a big one."

"Quite?" the girl screamed. "It's gigantic! I opened the window then I tried to tangle it up in this fluffy duster. It's legs just won't co-operate!"

"Better still – this." Philip took his damp towel from his shoulder and dropped it neatly over the creature. He scooped it up and carried it to the open window, where he shook it out vigorously, leaning as far forward as he could.

"All gone!" he announced to the girl, who was looking profoundly relieved.

"Thank you so much," she breathed, the colour returning to her face and a smile which made something inside him churn. "I think that deserves a drink, don't you? Would you like to ring my doorbell again in about an hour?"

As Philip made his way back to the lift, he thought he heard a chuckle close to his left ear. He turned his head quickly, but there was nobody there.

The Changelings

Miss Applebee picked up the house telephone. "Yes? Oh, Mrs Warlock's arrived, has she? Send her up to the drawing room, Edith, would you? Thank you."

She sat in an armchair by the window, where there stood a table and a smaller chair, and waited. In due course there came a discreet knock at the door.

"Come in!"

The door opened and a maid in cap and apron appeared, announcing, "Mrs Warlock, madam."

The woman who stepped into the room caused Miss Applebee to make an effort to hide her surprise and curiosity. Mrs Warlock presented a theatrical appearance bordering on the bizarre. A purple wide-brimmed hat was the focal point, beneath which hung a white lined face with fierce black eyebrows, at variance with the grey fuzzy hair straggling out from underneath. She wore a lilac coat with a large pink striped scarf flung around the shoulders, and she held a cavernous black bag clutched in black-gloved hands.

"Miss Applebee, I presume?" The voice was deep, almost caressing in its throaty smoothness.

Miss Applebee gave an involuntary shiver in spite of the spring warmth from the open window.

"Do come in, Mrs Warlock, and sit down," she said, indicating the smaller chair across the table. "You've come a long way." She glanced down at an open letter lying on the table. "From Shropshire, I see. You must be tired."

"I'm never tired." Mrs Warlock sat down and looked through the window. "Lovely garden. Who looks after it?"

"A man from the village, Bob Downs. He comes twice a week." Miss Applebee felt annoyance at being questioned by a prospective employee. "I have interviewed a number of applicants already, and there are one or two still to be seen. Perhaps you could tell me a little more about yourself? You say in your letter that you are an experienced housekeeper. That is good. But do you understand that I also require the successful applicant to act as a companion too? Have you experience of that?"

The other woman smiled, giving her a secretive look. "Oh yes," she said softly. "It's a speciality of mine."

"Really?" Miss Applebee had a fleeting image of Mrs Warlock performing a music hall act.

"Oh yes. There are many lonely people in this world. I am... drawn to them."

"So you have been a paid companion before?"

"Many times."

Miss Applebee felt a slight anxiety. "So – you didn't stay with them? Was there any reason for that?"

"Oh yes." The woman's voice became even smoother. "They died. They were all very old when I first came to them, you see. I pride myself on making their last days happy."

"Well, as you can see I am not exactly on my last legs, so all that will not apply. Sixty-two is not exactly decrepit, is it?"

"Oh, not at all."

"It's just that I have no family and am not particularly strong. I need someone kind and competent around the place. Can you cook?"

"Oh yes. I have a diploma. It's here in my bag, with all my references."

"Good. Edith has been doing her best, but cooking is not exactly her best skill. When she is on holiday I do my best to cook for myself, but frankly I thoroughly dislike it."

Mrs Warlock began to remove her black gloves with slow deliberate movements. "May I ask, Miss Applebee, what happened to your last companion?"

Miss Applebee swallowed her annoyance. "Oh, she left to housekeep for her widowed father. I miss her greatly."

"I'm sure you do. One gets attached, doesn't one?"

Miss Applebee studied the woman's face, noting the bright dark eyes which seemed to be growing larger.

There was knock at the door and the woman's eyes became normal. Edith came into the room dressed in outdoor clothes. "I'll be off then, madam," she said with a quick glance at the visitor.

"Oh yes, Edith. I do hope your mother will be better soon. Now don't think of returning until she is completely recovered."

"Thank you, madam. You'll be alright, won't you?"

"Yes of course, Edith. Now off you go or you won't catch the three-thirty. Write to me and let me know how your mother is getting on."

When Edith had left the room, Mrs Warlock dropped her gloves into her black bag, which she closed with a snap.

"I didn't realise that you had a maid, Miss Applebee. It wouldn't be just myself looking after you, then?"

"Oh no. Edith used to help my last companion with the preparation of meals, and a cleaning woman comes in on Mondays and Thursdays. She cleans the rooms in rotation, as this is such a large house. Edith does the dusting and tidying and sees to the laundry. She answers the doorbell and does many other things much too numerous to mention."

Mrs Warlock smiled, accentuating the thinness of her lips. "I could do all that. You wouldn't need anyone else."

"What?"

"Think of the money you would save. I could cook, clean, do anything around the house, I'm very strong."

"Oh, but you don't understand. Edith and Mrs Withers have been with me for years. I wouldn't dream of..."

Miss Applebee's gaze was caught and held by a glow coming from somewhere at the back of Mrs Warlock's dark eyes. She became suddenly very attentive to the way the woman was slowly pulling the scarf from around her shoulders, until it collapsed onto her lap, where it was folded with the long white fingers and dropped into the black bag to join the gloves.

Miss Applebee pulled herself together sharply. "...wouldn't dream of parting with them. Now, Mrs Warlock, what kind of cooking do you do?"

"What kind would you like?" The glow had departed from the woman's eyes. "French? Italian?"

"Oh no, nothing like that. Good plain English food, that's all. I am particularly fond of puddings like chocolate sponges, apple tart, that kind of thing."

"Good," smiled Mrs Warlock. "That would be no trouble at all. I prefer plain food. So much better for the digestion, don't you think?"

"Yes. Quite." Miss Applebee was experiencing a feeling of vague unease and a kind of confusion. She brushed her hand over her eyes and blinked. Mrs Warlock's eyes had begun to glow again. "Will it take long to dispose of your home in Shropshire?"

"Oh no." The woman's voice purred like a cat. "I've been living in rented accommodation. A single telephone call could dispose of that, with a cheque in the post in lieu of notice. Don't you worry about a thing."

"But what about your luggage, your personal things? You would have to go back for them, wouldn't you?"

"I have brought them with me. They are in the car."

The inside of Miss Applebee's head was swirling and plunging out of control. She fought for equilibrium. "But I haven't decided yet…"

Mrs Warlock's eyes held Miss Applebee's as in a vice. In a matter of moments it was all over.

***

A week later Edith returned to the house, puzzled and hurt by the letter of dismissal she carried in her bag. She let herself into the kitchen, then decided to go straight up to her room to change into her working clothes before announcing her return. She had noticed that something aromatic was cooking on the hob and assumed that, as it was one of Mrs Wilkins' days, the cleaner was helping Miss Applebee with the cooking.

She came back into the kitchen, intending to make morning coffee and take it up to her employer. Miss Applebee stood there with an apron tied around her waist, stirring the pot on the hob.

"Madam?"

Miss Applebee continued to stir without answering. Edith went to her and looked into her face. Miss Applebee's eyes were dull and vacant as she stared down at her task, ignoring the presence of the maid.

"Madam? What are you doing?"

"Making lunch." The voice was as dull as her eyes, almost robotic.

Edith was at a loss. "Where's Mrs Withers?"

"We dismissed her. And the gardener."

"What? Dismissed Mrs Withers and Bob after all these years? Why?"

"We thought it best. We didn't need them – or Edith."

An icy cold fear suddenly possessed Edith. "Madam, I'm Edith. Look at me, Madam – *look at me!*"

Miss Applebee turned and looked at Edith, but there was no recognition in her eyes. She could have been looking at a visiting stranger.

Miss Applebee put down the wooden spoon and went to the house telephone.

She dialled a number with slow mechanical movements. "Madam? Would you like custard or chocolate sauce with your sponge pudding? ...Chocolate sauce. Very well." Miss Applebee replaced the telephone and came back like a sleepwalker to continue stirring the pot. Edith stared in astonishment.

The front doorbell rang. Edith left the kitchen with a worried backward glance at Miss Applebee and went to answer the bell.

A middle-aged man stood on the doorstep holding a briefcase. "Good morning, Edith."

"Mr Walker! Oh, do come in – am I pleased to see you! To see anybody!"

"Really? Is something wrong? I came today because Miss Applebee rang to consult me about changing her will."

"*What*? Look. Would you mind coming with me to the kitchen, Mr Walker. I'll tell you something on the way."

During the walk to the kitchen, Mr Walker was appraised of an astonishing situation. When they arrived Miss Applebee was standing at the worktable assembling the ingredients for chocolate sauce. Mr Walker went to her and peered intently into her face.

"Good morning, Miss Applebee."

Miss Applebee turned to look at him but her eyes showed no recognition.

"Miss Applebee? You rang yesterday about changing your will?"

"Did I? Oh yes, so I did."

"And what exactly are the changes you wish to make, if I may ask?"

"Ah... er... oh yes. I wish to completely cut out Edith, Mrs Withers and Bob Downs. Oh, and my cousin in Bedford. Everything goes to Mrs Warlock. See to it, please – I have work to do." The voice was monotonous and mechanical and the eyes were devoid of expression.

Edith and Mr Walker looked at each other in horror, and then the house telephone rang. Edith automatically moved to answer but Miss Applebee was there before her. "Yes, madam? Yes, right away."

She walked past the other two and picked up the kettle. Pausing uncertainly, she turned to look at them.

"Madam wants her coffee. You must leave now."

"I think not," said Mr Walker calmly, taking the kettle from her and replacing it. "Madam will have to wait for her coffee. Edith, will you telephone the police and Miss Applebee's doctor?"

Miss Applebee had gone deathly pale. "But – I *must* make madam's coffee!" she said weakly.

"Why?" asked Mr Walker pleasantly. "What do you suppose might happen if you don't?"

"The devils! They'll come again! They're terrible, deadly things that will come in the night again. Give me that kettle!"

"Now, Miss Applebee, I want you to sit down in this chair and relax…"

"No, no! That's what she told me to do – then the devils came. I must never relax again… never relax… just work and be very, very quiet. Then they won't come, do you see?"

"Yes, I see," said Mr Walker soothingly. "Alright, put the kettle on if that's that you want to do."

Miss Applebee scuttled over to the sink and filled the kettle with shaking hands. Her distress was the first sign of animation they had seen in her.

Edith put the telephone down and came over to Mr Walker. "They're on their way," she whispered, and Mr Walker nodded.

The kitchen door, which had a slight creak, slowly opened. Mrs Warlock stood in the doorway, her face contorted with rage.

"So! I knew something was going on – you disappoint me, Jane. You have let me down, haven't you?"

"No, no, I haven't, madam! It's these people, not me!" Miss Applebee seemed terrified. "Look, I'm making your coffee for you – these people will all have to leave. I have already told them so."

Mrs Warlock stepped further into the kitchen, her eyes fixed on Miss Applebee. "Now what did I tell you about not letting anybody in unless I say so? Now you're going to die, and the devils will be with you for all eternity!"

Miss Applebee screamed and pressed back against the kitchen sink as Mrs Warlock snaked past Mr Walker in one swift movement, grabbing up a kitchen knife, which she raised above the frightened woman's head.

A shadow blocked out the daylight from the open back door, and then a gnarled hand grabbed Mrs Warlock's wrist from behind and twisted the knife from her hand. It fell to the floor at the same moment as Miss Applebee crumpled downwards in a dead faint.

"Bob!" cried Edith, letting out a great breath of relief. "Thank God you're here!"

"Come to see why I've been given the push after all these years, ain't I? Bloody good job too, by the look of things 'ere!"

***

The case became known as the Serial Hypnosis Murders. Mrs Warlock was found to have hypnotised a series of vulnerable elderly people who had no relatives, made them change their wills in her own favour and then killed them. She had brilliantly covered her tracks for a while, until her own diseased mind had finally begun to deteriorate and she had started to make mistakes, unable to think through practical details. Accounts deposited in different banks under different names had begun to coincide with the murders, and investigations had at last led the authorities onto the trail of Mrs Warlock. When she had arrived at the home of Miss Applebee, the police were already looking for her.

"So what'll 'appen to 'er then?" asked Bob some time later as he sat in the kitchen, having tea with Edith and Mrs Withers.

"Oh, she'll probably end up in Broadmoor," said Edith. "Mad as a hatter, of course."

"Didn't know we was all in Miss Applebee's will," said Mrs Withers. "Decent old stick, isn't she?"

"Yes, decent old stick," agreed Edith. "Do you know, she doesn't remember a thing about what happened?"

"What – none of it?"

"Nothing. I'm really glad about that. More tea, anyone?"

The Bytings

They were hot, tired and thirsty as they drove to the village of Lower Byting.

"Now to try and find the estate agent," sighed Sally Trench. "It's one thing to manage to get to a place, quite another to find anything when you get there."

"No, look – there's a pub. Let's have a cold drink and a sandwich first. I'm parched." Andy Trench spun the wheel and drew into the pub car park, switched off the engine and lay back with closed eyes. There were beads of sweat on his forehead and upper lip. His wife noticed.

"*Now* do you think it's a good idea to invest in an air-conditioned car? We can easily afford it with your retirement golden handshake and my mother's legacy. Just imagine, no more hot sweaty journeys in summer with the windows open and the draught blowing our heads off, not to mention the road noise."

"OK, OK. One thing at a time. Lunch first, then perhaps the people in the pub can tell us exactly where to find the agent. I just hope Upper Byting isn't too far away."

In the pub they seated themselves at a window overlooking a rose garden and applied themselves gratefully to ice-cold beer and sandwiches made with local ham.

"Jolly good ham," said Andy, forgetting his manners and speaking with his mouth full.

"Mm... mm!" Sally's eyes were half-closed with pleasure. "Wouldn't mind this pub being our local, would you?"

"Strange name," said Andy. "The Moon Dog. There's got to be a reason for that."

"Local legend, perhaps?"

"Maybe. I didn't notice the painting on the inn sign, did you?"

Sally considered. "Don't think I did. We'll look on the way out." She looked around her. "Lovely old pub. Low beams, ingle nook – I wonder if it's all genuinely old? Lots of them are pseudo. Ignoramuses like me can't tell the difference."

The landlord came to their table. "Everything alright?" he asked affably.

"Fine. Lovely ham," said Sally.

"Ah, that's our local stuff. Famous for miles around. You passing through or staying?"

"Just a day visit. We've come to view a cottage in Upper Byting we might be interested in. Incidentally, can you direct us to your estate agent called..."

"Marston," put in the landlord. "Ron Marston. He's the only one around here. He knows every brick of every house in both villages. He's just a few yards away. You just turn left out of here and walk a few shops along. It's next door to the butcher. You can leave your car in our parking if you like."

Ron Marston proved to be a bluff, genial man – a large man in a small man's body with an unexpectedly deep voice for his size. He had a monk-like ring of grey hair around a bald scalp and sported side-whiskers. Sally took to him on sight but Andy reserved judgement. "Hail-fellow-well-met type," Andy muttered when the agent had gone to find the cottage keys. "You have to watch that sort."

"Here we are then," said Mr Marston, bustling back. "Keys to Rabbits Cottage."

"Funny name," observed Sally, "what with the pub being called The Moon Dog. We looked at the inn sign a moment ago and couldn't quite make out what it's supposed to be. It looked at first like a small dog baying at the moon, but on a closer look it seemed like a small boy. Is there a story behind that?"

Mr Marston looked at them consideringly, then sat down behind his desk. "You'd better sit down again if you want the story. It also involves Rabbits Cottage."

The couple looked at each other, then at the agent before sitting.

"There's nothing wrong with the cottage itself, in fact it's a highly desirable property," said the agent, "but old tales tend to cling to it."

"It isn't haunted, is it?" said Sally quickly.

Mr Marston took on a guarded look. "People in the past have reported hearing voices. Some folk can be very imaginative about things like that. I'll fill you in on the background and let you decide." He grinned suddenly. "A fine way to sell a property!"

"I'd say it's rather a good gimmick," said Andy. "Personally I'm intrigued."

"Alright, I'll start at the beginning. Long ago these two villages were called Upper and Lower Marston."

"Like your name?" said Sally.

"Exactly. The Marston family have lived around here for generations. Still do, but there are not many of us left now. The original cottage was built in Upper Marston in 1784 by a reclusive scholar who didn't want any close neighbours. That's why it stands practically on the edge of the wood in splendid isolation. When the recluse died it was lived in by an ex-mercenary soldier and his wife and family. He had come back from foreign wars to settle here, but he had contracted an…illness…abroad and eventually died. Unfortunately he passed on the illness to his whole family. About that time there began to be rumours about the woods near the cottage. Strange animal noises were heard, rustlings in the undergrowth, a weird sort of howling at full moon."

"Is this a werewolf legend then?" asked Sally.

"Not exactly. One night, when the howling was particularly bad, a group of village men took up knives and cudgels and went to investigate the isolated cottage. There in the garden the youngest child, a boy, was crouching on all fours and shrieking at the moon. When he saw the men he rushed at them and bit one of them on the leg. The other men drove the boy back into the cottage and took the injured man home. The man became severely ill and died, foaming at the mouth."

"I think I can see where this is going," said Andy, darting a look at Sally.

"Then," continued Mr Marston, "strange things began to happen also down in Lower Marston. People attacked and then becoming ill. One by one the dead soldier's family died, but by then others had been infected and both villages became known as Upper and Lower Byting, and in time the name stuck. And the dead soldier's cottage came to be called Rabids Cottage."

"Which transmogrified into Rabbits Cottage?" said Sally.

"Quite. Then in 1801 it was bought by an elderly cleric who wanted a quiet retreat in which to write a book on church history. He kept the name for its quaintness – it was then still Rabids Cottage. When he realised that it was named after a nasty illness, that a whole family had suffered and died of rabies there, he had the whole place entombed in an outer layer of brick. Every inner wall and all the outer walls, the floors, the inside of the roof – the whole cottage was like a skeleton enclosed in new brickwork, with the exception of the roof which was closed off with timbers."

"I can see why he wanted to do that," said Andy, "but why didn't he simply move somewhere else?"

"Because he loved the location, the views from the windows and the isolation. He knew it was the right place to be for writing his book."

"That's a coincidence," said Sally. "Andy has begun to write a book too."

"Oh?" said the agent, looking at Andy with interest. "A novel?"

"Oh no, I don't do fiction. This one is about the history of the River Thames from the Middle Ages to the present day. I've been thinking about it and making notes for years. Now that I've retired I've got a real chance to get down to it. The cottage sounds perfect."

"Wait a minute – what about the voices people heard?" said Sally.

"Not all the occupiers heard them," said Mr Marston. "I rather think that they might have been influenced by hearing the stories about the place. However, if you would rather not see it…"

Sally and Andy looked at each other and nodded.

"Right." The agent stood and picked up the keys. "I'll drive you."

***

It was the following April before they moved into the cottage. Upper Byting proved to be smaller than Lower Byting and even more picturesque. The village had expanded over the years so that Rabbits Cottage was no longer standing in such isolation. The march of time had halted about fifty yards from the cottage, which still stood at the edge of the wood. Their only disappointment was that the public house was small and overcrowded, so they decided that the Moon Dog was to be their local hostelry.

"This is quite enough isolation for me," Sally said after the move. "Any more and I would have felt uneasy. I quite like the idea of that little police station being our nearest neighbours."

"Yes, and no more blaring noise from neighbours with their windows open in summer. Shall we get a dog?"

Sally hesitated. "I don't know."

"Why not?"

"I know it's silly, but... the history of this place... rabies and all that."

"Don't be so daft. There isn't any rabies flying about here after all this time. In any case you can only get it through a bite or some way of it getting into your blood stream. If you feel creepy about it, don't forget the walls of this place have all been cladded inside and out, so the original building is no more than a skeleton hidden away."

"Yes, I know. OK, let's get a dog. The grandchildren will love it. But only if I can have a cat. It will be just like old times when we were first married."

***

One hot night in July, Sally was having a sleepless night, She had gone to bed exhausted after having looked after two grandchildren for a week whilst her daughter and son-in-law had gone for a much-needed holiday in Tuscany. She had been having heavy nightmares and had woken up several times drenched in sweat and shuddering with horror. At last she got up and quietly went downstairs to the kitchen, avoiding the midway creaking stair.

She stood by the draining board and looked through the window at the night. The sky was clear and brightly studded with stars. There was moonlight, but the moon was out of sight behind the cottage. A fox shrieked eerily. As she looked she saw a small black shape streaking towards the house across the back garden and making for the annex utility room which they had built next to the kitchen. It was their cat, Judy who was being followed by a bigger black shape. Alarmed, and remembering the shriek of the fox, Sally ran to the door to the annex and wrenched it open.

In the dog basket, peacefully curled up asleep, was their yellow ragamuffin mongrel Punch, his untidy little-old-man face blissful. Then the cat flap burst open and Judy flung herself into the room, eyes staring and tail twice its size with terror. She was closely followed by a large black head with blazing eyes and ferocious teeth. Unluckily for the head it was too big to admit the rest of its owner, who upon seeing Sally tried to pull the head backwards to escape. Punch woke up, saw the intruder and began to bark hysterically. Judy, upon perceiving that human protection was nigh, turned to face the intruder and began to bravely hiss and spit, but the interloper's collar was too far through the cat flap and all its struggles were in vain.

The kitchen light was switched on and Andy came into the annex. "What the hell's going on here? You OK, Sal?"

"I'm OK, but *that* isn't," said Sally, pointing to the black face which had now lost its former ferocity and was now panting and lolling its red tongue.

"Oh. Right. I presume it's stuck then?"

"It was chasing Judy and it could have caught her. Look at the size of it – those teeth!"

Andy considered for a moment, then he took up a mop and advanced on the trapped head. The dog's eyes rolled anxiously. With the long mop-handle, Andy pushed and prodded until the dog's collar was far enough through the flap to enable the animal to free itself and disappear into the night.

"Ugly brute," commented Andy, replacing the mop and feeling that he had just performed one of the labours of Hercules and deserved a 'well done' at least.

"I'd never have thought of doing that," commented Sally admiringly. "Look, let's take the animals upstairs for tonight. See how upset they are." She swept Judy up into her arms. "This one's still trembling."

The next morning Sally told Andy about her night of bad dreams. "Every time I managed to drift off along came another one. It was as though the cottage was trying to tell me something. I felt so uneasy that I couldn't stay in bed a moment longer."

"Tell you what I think. The kids were too much for you in this hot weather and you were exhausted. Take it easy for a few days. We'll eat out tomorrow – how about the Moon Dog in Lower Byting? We can have a scrumptious ham salad."

Sally shuddered. "We had a moon dog of our own last night. Where on earth did that creature come from?"

"I phoned the police this morning before you were awake. They said it might have been a hunting dog belonging to poachers. They go into the woods sometimes to catch small deer and sell them on to hotels as venison. Judy must have wandered too near the woods. A hunting dog wouldn't have been able to resist chasing her."

"Those bad dreams – I thought I was being warned of something awful about to happen. And then the dog came through the cat flap."

"Just a coincidence."

Sally stirred her coffee and said nothing.

***

Andy had worked hard all through the spring and summer, taming the overgrown garden, weeding and pruning and planting. Sally had been able to preserve fruit from the bushes and trees and make jam, also to freeze Andy's runner beans. In quiet moments they read books borrowed from the small travelling library which visited from Lower Byting. Sally had booked herself in for a computer course in Lower Byting and Andy had begun to write his book in earnest. By that autumn they felt settled and happy.

"Do you want the car for anything?" Sally asked one day.

"No. Why?"

"Having made all that jam I'd now like to make some marmalade. I'm going to that nice greengrocer's for some Spanish oranges. I know it's not very far to that end of the village but it's begun to rain. Anything you want from the shops?"

"Yes. More paper for the printer."

"OK. Shan't be long. I'll make coffee when I get back."

Once alone, Andy turned back to his computer and became lost in work. A few minutes had passed when he began to feel unwell. He was sweating and shivering and felt curiously thirsty. Alarmed, he went to the kitchen for a glass of water. He took a glass from a cupboard and approached the sink. As the water flowed from the tap some of it splashed his hand. He cried out and sprang backwards, horrified at the thought that the water might touch him. In spite of burning thirst he knew that if he tried to swallow water he would suffocate. Dazed, he sank to the floor as his knees gave way. He sat with his back against the sink unit, clutching an empty glass and tormented with thirst.

Punch trotted into the kitchen and saw Andy sitting on the floor, which was usually a prelude to a joyful game of wrestling and tickling. He leapt happily upon his master, whereupon Andy shrieked and pushed him away. Puzzled and disappointed the dog went into the annex and flopped into his basket.

Andy crawled on his hands and knees into the living room still clutching the glass. He hauled himself up onto the couch and lay there exhausted. He drifted into an uneasy sleep and dreamed of voices crying to him from the walls.

"Are you alright, Andy?"

He woke with a start to see Sally bending over him. He looked around him and blinked. "Yes, fine. Must have drifted off." He was too confused to tell her anything.

"I peered into the study on my way in but you weren't there. You hadn't switched your computer off. You seem to have written something odd, not in keeping with the book you're writing. Look – I've printed it out."

Andy took the paper and looked. It read: LET US OUT LET US OUT LET US OUT.

"I didn't write this."

"Well, I certainly didn't."

Andy sat up with difficulty. All his previous sick feelings had gone, leaving him washed out and lethargic. What remained was the thirst. He held up the glass. "Be an angel and get me a drink of water, Sal."

Sally took the glass and gave him a curious look before going to the kitchen. While she was gone Andy studied the paper thoughtfully, remembering his feverish dream.

When Sally came back he took the glass and drained all the water in one go. "I couldn't have done that a while ago," he said, wiping his mouth with the back of his hand.

"What? Why not?"

"While you were out I began to feel very ill. Sort of feverish and shaky, horrible painful feelings and a truly terrible thirst. I managed to get to the kitchen but when I turned on the tap I couldn't bear the thought that the water might touch me."

"But – that's just like..."

"Yes. Then I managed to get myself to this room and onto the couch, but I felt dreadful. I fell asleep and had a sort of nightmare. There were voices calling to me from behind these walls."

Sally sat beside him and was quiet for a moment, then she said, "Do you remember the night the black dog came through the cat flap?"

"Who could forget?"

"Well... before that I had been having a nightmare. I dreamed that the cottage was trying to tell me something. I didn't exactly hear voices but I felt that some terrible emotion had been trapped here. In my dream I thought I could make a hole in one of the walls and let it out, whatever it was." She picked up the paper again. "Let us out, it says here. What's going on, Andy?"

The next day there were ten jars of marmalade standing in the kitchen neatly capped and labelled. The sunlight shining through them made pools of gold on the table top.

Andy came in from the annex and sniffed appreciatively. "Lovely fruity smell!"

"Andy..."

"What?"

"What do you think about this place? Do you think we should move?"

"Do you?"

"I don't want to. Everything here is so perfect. The garden, the woods, the village. We've made friends here, you're writing, I'm doing yoga and computer studies – it's just this strange stuff that's going on."

"Maybe there's something we can do about it."

"Such as?"

"I've been thinking. When I was in the Moon Dog last week the landlord was telling me that there was a sort of... woman... here in Upper Byting."

"Yes, there are quite a lot of us around here."

"Don't be sarky. This one's special. I suppose in bygone days she'd have been called a witch, or the village wise woman."

Sally looked at him wide-eyed.

"So," continued Andy, not returning her look. "I thought maybe she could come here and give the place the once-over. Can't do any harm, can it?"

"And do what exactly?"

"I can't say exactly. But the landlord told me that she was good at clearing houses of unwanted atmospheres – influences and suchlike."

"What, like ghostbusters?"

Andy shrugged. "Apparently her grandmother was a medium and so was her mother. This woman isn't, but she's something or other along those lines. Shall I give her a ring?"

"Do you know her number?"

"I know her name – Martha Penn. She'll be in the phone book."

Sally was silent for a moment, then, "OK. She's probably quite mad but what have we got to lose? We can't both be going off our heads. There's definitely something going on here."

***

The woman who had rung the doorbell was standing a little way back, scanning the cottage walls. She was short and plump with round glasses and very black close-cropped hair. She was neatly dressed and could have passed for a teacher or a company secretary. Sally felt slightly disappointed, having expected something more bizarre.

"Mrs Penn?" said Sally. "Do come in."

"Thank you – and it's Miss."

"Oh, sorry. Andy, Miss Penn's here!"

When they were all seated in the lounge, Judy strolled in and sat in the middle of the floor contemplating the company with half-closed yellow eyes. Suddenly her eyes widened and she looked intently to her left, then she relaxed again with just a flick of the tail.

"Does the cat often do that?" asked Miss Penn.

Sally felt slightly irritated. "All cats do that most of the time."

"Of course," said Miss Penn evenly. "But this one is picking up on something."

Sally and Andy exchanged glances – Sally's anxious and Andy's interested.

Miss Penn looked around the room. "I'm just going to close my eyes. Would you please not talk for a moment?"

There was silence in the room, during which Judy jumped up on to Miss Penn's ample lap and curled up in a ball, purring. Miss Penn showed no surprise.

"Right." Miss Penn opened her eyes, her fingers sensuously touching the cat's fur. "I'm now going to ask you both if you would mind going outside the house for a short while. I need to assess the situation alone. I've waited a long time to see the inside of this place."

Reluctantly they rose to leave through the French windows. "Come on, Judy!" called Sally.

"NO! She stays," stated the visitor flatly.

Once in the back garden Sally exploded. "Well! I've never before been ordered about in my own home!"

"Never mind," placated Andy. "She's doing a job for us. We did invite her, didn't we?"

"Yes, but... is she genuine?"

"Who knows? Let's go and see how the garden looks today."

There were bees buzzing in the lavender bushes. Sally stood still and looked down at them, soothed as always by the sound. Birds flew overhead, making for the wood.

Just as Sally was about to remark on the peace of the garden the French windows flew open and Miss Penn staggered out into the garden, sinking to her knees and clutching her throat. The others ran to her and lifted her onto a wooden bench.

"Miss Penn! Whatever's the matter?" said Sally, really frightened.

"It's alright," said Andy calmly. "She's experiencing the same thing that happened to me. Now take it easy, Miss Penn. It will soon go away."

"Yes, I do know that," gasped Miss Penn. "Just give me a few minutes. It's the house, you see. It's waking up."

"What on earth do you mean?" demanded Sally, anxiety making her tense.

Miss Penn took a deep breath, then let it out noisily. "There! It's gone. Shall we go back inside?"

When they were seated in the lounge with cups of coffee, Miss Penn was ready to talk. "Now, tell me – have either of you had unpleasant experiences?"

"Yes. I had a very similar one to yours," said Andy. "Feverish ill feelings, pain, mad thirst."

"Exactly." Miss Penn turned to Sally. "And you, my dear?" Her tone was kindly, almost motherly.

Sally thought back to her night of bad dreams. "Well... some time ago I had a nightmare when I thought there was something in the walls trying to get out. It was quite horrific at the time, one of those sweaty dreams. I had the mad idea that I could make a hole in the wall and let it out."

Miss Penn put down her cup and looked around the room. "Exactly right," she said softly. "The walls. You know the history of this place, of course? People experienced great suffering here in the past. A horrible incurable disease sent them mad. Walls absorb emotions, but sooner or later these feelings must be released. This has never happened properly here. I take it these are not the original walls?"

"That's right," said Andy. "The old house is completely hidden by later walls, inside and out. The whole place has three thicknesses of wall. Cool in summer, warm in winter."

"So there lies the problem and the solution. What is inside has to be let out."

"Wait a minute," said Sally. "We've only recently had the whole place redecorated. We're certainly not taking any walls down."

Miss Penn gave a wide smile, making deep dimples appear around her mouth. "You don't have to. It's much simpler than that. You have already dreamt the solution."

"What?"

"Make a hole somewhere, that's all. Make sure it includes both outer and inner walls. And change the name of this cottage."

"Oh no, not again!" Andy groaned. "We've been through all that already with the move – bank, pension, investments, gas, water, electricity..."

"Rabbits Cottage was born out of Rabids Cottage. You must change it. Let nothing of the past remain."

Sally looked around the room. "So what has caused all this to happen to us?"

"You caused it, my dear?"

"What? I caused it? How?"

"You woke the house up. For all your scepticism you are a natural sensitive. You have the gift. Did you not know that?"

"Sorry, I can't believe that."

"Nevertheless, it's true. There may come a time when you will be glad of it. And now I think there is something else you want to tell me?" Miss Penn looked from one to the other of them and waited calmly.

Reluctantly Andy felt in his pocket and drew out the printout of the strange words. "Here, take a look at this. What do you make of it?"

Miss Penn took the paper and studied it. "Where did this come from?"

They told her the story, Sally scrutinising the woman's face, trying to read her reaction.

"Yes... well... this only reinforces my reading of the situation." Miss Penn stood up and handed the paper back. "And now I shall leave you to do what you have to do. Make those holes today. An upper room would be best, facing east. Call me if you ever need more advice."

"Wait a minute," said Andy, following the woman to the door. "What about your fee?"

"What fee? I have never polluted my gift with money."

They had reached the front door and Andy opened it. They all shook hands as Judy darted into the garden.

"Fine cat," remarked Miss Penn. "I've always liked the black ones best. Goodbye!"

"I'll bet she does," giggles Sally. "Wonder if she's got a cauldron? Or a broomstick to fly off to Hogwarts?"

Andy waved the paper in Sally's face. "What about this then? Let us out and all that? Did you type this?"

"No, of course not!"

"Quite. Neither did I. And the weird things did happen, didn't they?"

"Well – yes."

"So let's do what Miss Penn suggested, yes?"

"OK, OK! I'm a bit unsettled by being told I've 'got the gift'. Anyone would be. How would you like it?"

"I'd be fascinated."

"Are we going to change the name then?"

"You are. You're the one with the gift. Let's go and sit down and concentrate on a new name."

They returned to the living room and sat on the couch side by side.

"Close your eyes and think of something really nice," suggested Andy.

"Alright, the garden. Flowers. Grass. Apple tree. Plum tree. Rockery. Your runner bean plot. Lavender... bees... buzzing." Sally's eyes opened. "Got it – Lavender Cottage!"

"Couldn't be better." Andy stood up and stretched. "Well, before all the bother of changing our address yet again, I'm going to the garage to fetch my electric drill and use the longest bit I can find."

"You're really going to do it then?"

"Oh yes. I don't ever want that rotten experience again. I've never felt so ill in all my life. Whatever old resonances you've tickled up here, I'm going to give them an escape route. The box room faces east, I'll do it there."

Sally stood up. "What I don't understand is why can't all these spooky whatsits just go by themselves? It they are so insubstantial and ghostly surely mere brick walls couldn't contain them? Why do they need something as crude as your electric drill to release them?"

"Yes..." Andy scratched his head. "I must admit I don't feel too comfortable with that one myself. On the other hand it's been believed for centuries that buildings retain remnants of past events, especially really bad ones. Why haven't they released themselves? Perhaps it takes something just a bit more concrete, plus the presence of someone like you..."

"Like me? Oh, you mean what Miss Penn said. Well, I suppose we'd better get on with it, then."

Trying not to think of two or three practical objections to drilling the walls, Sally collected up the coffee things and took them back to the kitchen, where she washed the mugs and put them away. Then, feeling curiously peaceful, she went into the back garden followed by the animals and looked up at the box room window.

Andy appeared and opened the window. "Ah, there you are. I shall want you to tell me when you see the drill bit coming through. OK?"

The noise of the drilling continued for some time, then Andy looked down and called, "Anything?"

"Can't see a thing yet!"

The drilling began again. Sally watched and eventually saw some little puffs of dust coming from the outer wall. She waited until the noise stopped, and then she called up to Andy. He appeared with his hair covered in white dust.

"Anything?"

"Yes, you're coming through. Lots of dust. You must be nearly there."

After a few minutes of more drilling there was a sudden minor avalanche of bits and pieces of small rubble tumbling down onto the path below.

Andy looked out of the window. "Am I there yet?"

"Eureka! I'm coming up!"

In the box room Sally saw with dismay the damage to the plaster and the rubble on the floor. She glanced at the hole in the wall. "What's to stop damp coming into the room with that thing there?"

"Well, I'm hardly going to leave it like that, am I? I'll simply plaster over this side. I can fix a fine metal mesh over the outside hole. It can act as an air brick. Now let's hope Miss Penn is right and we're free of all that business."

"Right. Now for your next job..."

Andy groaned.

"...perhaps you can make a new name sign for Lavender Cottage."

"Listen!" Andy put his head on one side straining to hear something. "What's that noise?"

At first Sally heard nothing, until she became aware of a vibration in her head accompanied by a low humming sound. She put both her hands over her head and looked around the room. The vibration seemed to be coming from the walls, and glancing at Andy she saw that he too was holding his head and screwing up his face. Sally went to the window and looked out.

"Andy – come and look at this!"

They saw that both animals had rushed back into the garden and were behaving strangely. Punch was shaking his head and leaping about whilst Judy was crouched and energetically wiping a paw over one ear. Then the sound ceased as suddenly as it started and the silence was profound.

"Gone, do you think?" whispered Andy.

"Absolutely. Goodbye Rabbits Cottage."

"Hello Lavender Cottage. Now let's get cleaned up and go down to the Moon Dog before we do anything else here. We'll have a celebration drink and a nice meal."

Sally sighed happily. "And when we come back it will be our first real homecoming. The place belongs to us."

***

When they arrived at the Moon Dog there was a small crowd collected on the pavement outside, including the landlord. A police car drew up and the local sergeant got out and joined the crowd, who were all looking up at the inn sign.

Andy parked the car and they both hurried around to the front of the pub. The sergeant was looking up at the inn sign and looking as puzzled as everyone else.

"What's wrong?" Andy asked a man in the crowd.

"Look!" The man pointed upwards. "See?"

They pushed their way towards where the sergeant and the landlord were standing and peered up at the sign. Where the figure of the crouching boy had been there was a blank space showing the mottled wood beneath, in the exact shape of the boy howling at the moon.

"Why should anyone want to do such a thing?" the landlord was saying to the police officer. "And in broad daylight! Nobody saw anything happening and as far as anybody knew there haven't been any of those townie yobs around all day."

The sergeant squinted upwards. "Doesn't look like the work of yobs anyway. They would be too crude to make such a precise job of it. Are you sure it wasn't done at night by some nutter?"

"No. It was fine this morning. My barman said as he came in that he thought the sign could do with a good clean, so we know everything was alright then. The boy seems to have just suddenly disappeared. To take away the boy would have needed a long ladder and a precision job. What's going on here!"

Andy and Sally looked at each other and said nothing, then made their way into the Moon Dog. When they were seated at a table Andy let out a long breath.

"If only they knew," said Sally. "It was us, of course, wasn't it?"

"What else? Now there's nothing left except the name of this pub. Maybe they'll change it now."

Andy picked up the menu and felt in his jacket pocket for his reading glasses. As he pulled them out a piece of folded paper fell on to the table. He took it and unfolded it. He looked at it, then silently handed it to Sally.

"There's nothing on it."

"Exactly. That's the piece of paper you printed out from the computer. All the letters have vanished. Final closure, do you think?"

Sally nodded.

Murder Most Fouled-Up

Julia Taylor had perfected the art of watching people without appearing to have noticed them, of listening to other people's conversations without seeming to hear them. It enriched her rather dull life and put colour into what she called her 'beige' existence. In her spare time she lived vicariously through characters in novels, films and television plays. At work in her job of filling shelves in a supermarket, she had ample opportunity of tuning into snatches of talk or of noting variants like age, dress or attitude.

It was with something of a shock that she overheard a murder being plotted. At first she was astonished then, when the reality kicked in, desperately worried.

It started with the older grey-haired man saying, as he reached up for a bottle of pesto after a furtive looked around, "When are you going to kill her, then?"

The younger man, dark and pleasant-looking, also gave a quick look around before replying, "Thursday night."

"You mean Thursday this week?"

"Yes. Keep your voice down. I planned it months ago."

"About time too, son. Dangerous, nasty woman. I don't know how you've managed to put up with her for so long. I'd have snuffed her out long ago."

"Thanks, Dad. Knew you'd be on my side. They've got quite a decent café in this shop. Fancy a cup of tea?"

The two men moved away, chatting amiably, leaving Julia gasping. As it was time for her break, she went along to the café where she stood looking around at the tea drinkers and bun eaters. She spotted the two men at a window table, then she ordered tea and chocolate biscuits before seating herself at the next table, her well-trained ears alert. She took a notebook and pen from her overall pocket and fell to gazing innocently through the window.

"I agonised over the decision," the young man was saying. "You can't do that sort of thing lightly."

"Of course you can't, son," said the older man soothingly. "Takes guts."

"Her family will miss her. You know how her father dotes on her. He doesn't seem to have the slightest idea of what she's really like. I feel a bit guilty."

"Don't, son! Look at the way she forced her daughter from her first marriage to give up her boyfriend – nearly committed suicide over that, the poor girl. And what about the time she poisoned the cat next door? No, don't you feel guilty about removing that one. She's ruined more than one person's life. The world will be a better place."

Julia's heart raced as she scribbled furiously in her notebook. She jumped nervously when her tea and biscuits arrived.

"Writing a book, then?" grinned the waitress.

"What? Oh, thanks, Gladys. Those don't look like chocolate biscuits."

"Only had ginger left. Sorry."

Left to herself, Julia resumed her listening, fuming at the interruption.

"I was going to push her downstairs at first," said the young man casually, stirring his tea, "then I wondered if I could run her over in a car. Finally I decided to set the Rottweiler on her. No fingerprints, no clues – perfect."

"How can you be sure that would work?"

"Jason's an ex-police dog. He'll do anything I say. Going for someone he thinks is a miscreant is second nature to him. All I have to do is encourage him to go just that little bit further."

"If it works out, you know you'll have to lose the dog, don't you? The police are very down on people who don't keep dangerous dogs under control."

The young man shrugged. "I can always get another dog."

The callousness appalled Julia. The pen slipped from her fingers and rolled away, ending up under the table of the two men, She froze.

The young man scrabbled under the table, straightened up and held out the pen. "This yours, miss?"

Julia reached out and took the pen with shaking hands. "Thanks," she whispered, noting the nice brown eyes and friendly smile.

The young man turned back to his father and continued their conversation, albeit in more of an undertone which challenged Julia's sharp hearing. "It has to look like an unfortunate piece of carelessness," he said as he buttered a slice of toast. "The dog doesn't like her. That will help."

The older man sighed. "Well, if your mind's made up..."

"It's all set up, Dad, down to the last detail. Don't ask me to explain it all now." The young man stirred his tea thoughtfully. "You never liked her, did you?"

"No, Ed, I thought she was the greatest mistake you ever made. She changed everything somehow, and other people agreed with me. She hurt and upset far too many people. Nice people, harmless people. Even her own family. I'm not surprised her first husband ran off with another woman. I'll never know how she managed to con into marriage..."

"Don't, Dad!" groaned the young man, putting one hand over his eyes.

"I suppose it was her looks?"

"Isn't it always? She couldn't even cook. That was why she forced her daughter to study cookery, so she didn't have to do it herself."

"Poor little Stephanie. As I remember, she only wanted to do hairdressing."

"Well, let's not talk about it anymore. I'm sick of the whole thing. I'll be glad when Thursday is over and I can put the whole sordid episode behind me. Glad you're backing me up, Dad. Now for more pleasant things – who's going to win the match on Saturday?"

"Man United, of course."

"What? Traitor! Never! Want to bet on it?"

***

Julia rushed home to her bedsit that evening and sat down with her notebook. As she scanned her scrawled handwriting she felt hot and agitated, then she put her powers of observation to the test by writing down the appearances of the two men in as much detail as she could remember. Only when she was completely satisfied with her work did she pick up the telephone to ring the police.

"Alright, madam," said a bored voice at the other end. "We'll send a couple of officers round to see you immediately." Julia did not hear him mutter, "Another nutter on the line."

Later, two plain-clothes officers were seated side by side on Julia's couch drinking tea and listening politely to her story.

"OK then, Miss Taylor," said one of the men, putting down his cup. "Could we see your notes?"

Julia handed the notebook over. "Sorry about the first part being so scrawled, but I don't know shorthand and I was trying to get it all down. You'll find the descriptions much easier to read. I did that when I got home and…"

"Right then, we'll take this back to the station and we'll be in touch. Thanks for the tea."

"Oh – one more thing! From where I sat I could see the car park. I saw them drive off."

"Oh? Can you describe the car?"

"Er – it was a blue one."

"A blue one." The officers exchanged a glance. "Can you be more specific? The make, perhaps?"

Julia blushed hotly. "I don't know about cars. Darkish blue, four wheels and a windscreen, that's about my limit. Oh, and the number."

"The number. Now you're talking." The officer pulled out his own notebook. "Yes?"

Julia rapped out the number, triumphant after the ignominy of the blue car.

"Thank you, Miss Taylor. As we said, we'll be in touch."

***

Julia heard nothing more for a couple of days. Thursday had come and was almost over, and she worried horribly. However awful that woman might have been, murder was murder and today was the day.

Her evening meal was over and she was about to wash the dishes when the doorbell rang. She opened the front door to find the same officers standing and looking at her with grim expressions, which made her catch her breath.

"Do you mind if we come in?" said one officer.

When the men were seated, one leaned forward and said, "Did you know that wasting police time is an offence?"

"Of course I do. What's that got to do with me?"

"We'll show you, Miss Taylor. Would you please switch on your television."

"What? Why?"

"Just switch it on, please," said the man, mentioning a channel number.

Puzzled, Julia went to the television and switched on, and then came back and sat down. "There you are then, an advert telling you how to get rid of your wrinkles. OK, what now?"

"Wait and see."

In silence the three of them watched until the advertising finished and a long-running soap appeared.

"I never watch this one," remarked Julia. "It's always at the same time as my favourite."

"Just hang on a bit."

Resigned, Julia sat back in her armchair and watched the screen. Presently the scene changed to a woman coming along a dark street and opening a garden gate. As she approached a house front, a huge black Rottweiler charged forward and knocked her over. She tried to fight it off but it pinned her to the ground and appeared to sink its teeth into her throat. There was a fade-out, then the same scene reappeared but with police cars and a covered body being carried towards an ambulance. Then the scene cut to a two-shot of a young girl and a man standing together in the same front garden. The girl was staring at the man with a horrified expression. She whispered fiercely, "You murderer! I know what you did! You killed my mother with your rotten dog!"

One of the police officers rose and switched off the television. He turned to face Julia, who was sitting white-faced with her hand to her mouth.

"I think you owe the scriptwriter an apology, Miss Taylor. Here's his telephone number. It's a Mr Edward Broad. We nearly arrested him. Goodnight, Miss Taylor. Sleep well."

A Tree, A Serpent And A Staff

Something magical has happened to me. Now don't get me wrong. I am by no means an over-imaginative man. As a respected chartered accountant I can't afford to be too fanciful, although as a mathematician I fully appreciate the exquisite precision underlying the cosmos.

I developed a distressing skin condition which gave me a permanently red face and neck. Nothing seemed to help. My doctor had told me the condition could well have a psychological basis and that maybe I should consult a psychiatrist. No way, I told him. Finally I accepted the situation and took to cover-up make-up, which was infinitely better than going about looking scarlet with embarrassment, although it was difficult to keep my collars clean.

Recently I went with my wife Anne on holiday to Greece – the island of Kos to be precise. The hot sunshine was a delight after a rather cold English spring, but it made my make-up run.

One day we discovered a square with an enormous and very old plane tree and we sat near it drinking wine and studying our guide book. As we read we discovered that the old tree was traditionally supposed to be the very tree under which the father of Greek medicine, Hippocrates, taught his students.

"When was that then?" said Anne, peering at the book over my shoulder.

"It says here that he was born in 460 BC and died 377 BC."

"Heavens!" exclaimed Anne, turning to look at the tree. "No wonder it needs propping up with all that scaffolding."

I looked at her scornfully. "Do you really suppose that tree to be more than two thousand years old?"

She looked at the tree thoughtfully. "Might be the same place though. The tree might be a descendent of the original."

"And pigs might fly. It makes a jolly good tourist attraction. But here's an interesting bit of info. Did you know that the Hippocratic Oath that doctors used to swear before they began to practise was in fact not written by Hippocrates?"

"So who did write it?"

"It doesn't say. But here's something else. You can book an excursion to a place outside town called the Asklepiion – that's also to do with ancient Greek medicine, it seems. It says here that there was a Greco-Roman god of medicine called Asklepios – there seem to be different spellings – who was the son of Apollo and the nymph Coronis."

"Those gods seem to have had a rollicking good time."

"Anyway, this place seems to have been built in his honour. His cult originated in Thessaly and spread throughout Greece. The place is a ruin, of course. Shall we go? We can book through the hotel."

The day of the excursion seemed hotter than ever. I was wearing a sun hat with a wide brim, but I envied Anne the umbrella she was using as a sunshade. The ruin we had come to see seemed to shimmer in the heat as our young guide gathered us around to introduce us to our subject.

"These ruins," she began in loud clear tones, "were in the beginning dedicated to Asklepios,, or Aesculapius to give him his Roman name, who was the ancient Greco-Roman god of healing. You may have seen pictures of his supposed likeness holding a staff with a snake coiling upwards around it. In the Sussex town where I live there is a symbol on the roof of the local hospital depicting a snake coiling around a staff. This symbol appears throughout the medical world... yes sir? You wanted to ask a question?"

"Yes!" A young man stepped forward. "What exactly is the purpose of this place?"

"I am, of course, coming to that," said the guide politely, although she looked slightly annoyed. "It was a kind of sanatorium, as were similar buildings elsewhere. This one is where Herodicus taught Hippocrates medicine. Asklepios was believed to put his patients into individual cells and leave them there to 'dream their healing'. We can only assume he taught them a kind of meditation on whatever part of the body was in need of healing... Yes?"

The young man had stepped forward again. "How could a god, a mythical figure, have put real people into cells?"

The guide looked momentarily panicky, then she smiled sweetly at her interrogator. "You tell me," she shrugged. "I'd rather like to know that myself. And now, if you would like to follow me, we will walk around and see everything a little closer."

"That puts him in his place," muttered Anne.

"Yes," I said, "there's always one. I was wondering if Asklepios started as a real person, then as time rolled by he began to be thought of as a god. You never know, do you?"

"Like being deified?"

"Why not? Seems logical to me."

As we walked the guide continued to talk. "Hippocrates, thought to be the father of Greek medicine, believed that disease was caused by the excreted vapours of undigested food."

The young man snorted in derision. The ear lobes of the guide turned pink.

"The philosophy of Hippocrates was to see the body as a whole – perhaps what we would today call holistic medicine."

"Ha!" exclaimed the young man. "Then maybe he should be called Hippycrates?"

A few people in the group tittered whilst others seemed irritated.

"Oh dear," said Anne. "The girl's doing her best. Why doesn't he shut up?"

"With any luck somebody might give him a smack round the ear," I muttered.

Halfway into the tour, as the guide enlightened us with her extensive knowledge, the young man spoke again.

"I say, miss – one more question?"

Some people in the group groaned but the young man stood his ground.

"Yes?" said the guide, stopping to look at her tormentor. There were icy glints in her smile.

"How do we know all this is true? Where does all this stuff come from?"

The guide lifted her clipboard high in the air in triumph. "Encyclopaedia Britannica – museums – libraries – computers – and going on courses. OK?"

With one accord the group clapped and one person cheered.

"I almost feel sorry for him now," whispered Anne as the young man gave a weak smile of defeat and hid behind a woman with a large sunshade.

Later, after walking right around the ruin, the group split up and sat on the grass to rest. We sat on the shady side to protect my make-up which was beginning to feel sticky and uncomfortable. I closed my eyes and dozed, trying to remember as much as I could of the guide's information.

"Oh, look!"

I opened my eyes. Anne was looking across the grass and I followed her gaze.

"Would you believe that?" she exclaimed.

I saw the guide sitting with her back against a large stone, whilst the tiresome young man sat close to her on the grass, his hands clasped around his knees. They were chatting amiably and laughing.

"Well I'll be... how could that happen?" I said.

"Don't you see? He fancied her."

"But – he was needling her all the time."

"That's right."

"What?"

"It was an opening gambit, don't you see?"

"No."

"Oh, go back to sleep. I'll join you. They'll call us when the coach is ready."

The heat was making me sleepy again. I closed my eyes and let my mind drift. The young guide's words floated in and out of my awareness. I thought of how those long-ago sick people slept alone to 'dream their healing'. What were they doing? What knowledge had the god given them?

I imagined myself to be alone in a dark enclosed space. I let my mind rest on bodily sensations. After a while I became acutely aware of the burning discomfort of my rash. Something prevented me from opening my eyes. I seemed to know it was important to remain steadily in that quiet state, aware only of my discomfort. Gradually the burning sensation began to diminish. I relaxed and drifted into a deep sleep, wondering at the relief.

I was just surfacing from sleep when I was aware of the merest whisper of a tingle most delightfully seeping along my spine. When I tried to hold onto the sheer delight of it, it faded beyond feeling and was lost.

Anne nudged me. "Come on – the coach driver's ready."

The group climbed into the coach in a rather disorderly fashion and Anne and I became separated. I found myself sitting next to the guide, much to the chagrin of the pestilential young man who was sitting beside Anne.

"Thank you for a fascinating talk," I said to the guide. "You must have done reams of research."

"You have to in my job. You can so easily be caught out by know-it-alls."

"Tell me about that staff of Asklepios with the snake. It must signify something."

She hesitated for a moment, then, "Well, I do have my own ideas about that. But I shouldn't really incorporate them in my official guide."

"But the tour is over. I'm just someone asking you a question apart from all that"

"OK. I have a personal theory, for what it's worth." Again she hesitated. "Strictly off the record?"

"Oh, absolutely."

After a pause she said, "Well, just think about it. A staff with a snake coiling upwards along it, held by a master of medicine. What does that say to you?"

"Nothing."

"Do you know anything about yoga?"

"Not much. All those strange postures."

"There's more than that. In ancient India there were tantric forms of yoga where it was believed that there was cosmic energy within everyone. This energy was imagined to be in the form of a snake coiled up at the base of the spine. Practices of meditation, exercises, etc, induced this energy to travel up the spine and in time reach the top of the head. That was supposed to bring complete enlightenment and a permanent state of bliss. The snake represented this energy. It was called Kundalini."

I was fascinated but cautious. "But Asklepios was a Greek god, as far as I know not connected with India."

"How do we know that? In the ancient world there *was* such a thing as travel, you know. Different cultures influenced each other all the time. Who can say that the cult of Asklepios didn't absorb something from the Vedic knowledge of ancient India?"

For a moment I felt a subtle frisson of excitement. I remembered my dream and thought about telling her, but decided against it. Some things are too fragile for exposure. I changed tactics.

"What about Asklepios putting patients in rooms to dream their healing? Maybe he wasn't a god at all, but some medicine man who knew something about human psychology, the mind-body connection? And perhaps he became a god as time passed."

The guide gave me an interested look. "You seem as fond of theorising as I am." she laughed.

I glanced over my shoulder to where Anne was sitting. "Do you mind awfully if I rescue my wife from your young man?"

"My what?" the guide exclaimed, but she had turned a delicate and most becoming shade of pink.

"I could take his place if you wouldn't mind the little pest taking mine?"

She shrugged, feigning nonchalance but not succeeding.

Back in the hotel, Anne and I kicked off our shoes and rested on our beds before the evening meal. I immediately fell asleep and had the most refreshing slumber I had experienced for many years, until Anne woke me.

"Wake up, George! It's time to get ready for dinner. You'll have to take off that streaky make-up and re-do it. It didn't do very well in that hot sun, did it?"

I carefully removed the old make-up and was about to apply more when I caught sight of myself in the mirror. I stared hard, blinked and stared again. The skin of my face and neck was pinkish-white – in other words perfectly normal. My knees suddenly became quite weak and I had to sit on a stool for a few moments.

I came back into the bedroom where Anne was sitting at the dressing table, trying to manipulate the catch on her necklace. "Come and fasten this silly thing for me, will you?"

I bent down to fasten the necklace behind her neck. She caught sight of me in the mirror and peered intently. "Are you using a different make-up? It looks quite natural, much better than usual."

"I'm not wearing any."

"What?"

"I'm not wearing any make-up. This is the real me."

For a moment she was speechless, then, "Well – hello real you. Whatever has happened?"

"I'm wondering that myself. Let's hope it lasts, whatever it is. Just think – no more dirty collars."

I told her nothing about my dream. I certainly didn't tell my doctor when I paid him my next visit.

"These psychosomatic conditions sometimes seem to have a will of their own," said my doctor, peering at my face. "Let's be thankful yours has gone. Well done you!"

My gaze fell on a printed information sheet lying on his desk. At the top of the sheet I saw a logo. It depicted a snake coiling around a staff.

"Yes," I murmured. "Well done me."

Finding Sparkie

A faint smell of burning emanated from the kitchen. Jane looked at the clock, swore under her breath and dashed for the kitchen, where she wrenched open the oven door. The edges of the pie were beginning to blacken.

"Right!" she muttered. "Stewart or no Stewart, the veggies are going on now. If necessary I'll eat alone. Nobody stands me up, especially when I take the trouble to cook for them."

***

Stewart had been on his way to Jane's flat and had gone into an Off Licence for a bottle of wine as a contribution towards the meal. His gaze idled along the shelves of bottles and eventually landed on the only other customer, a young man about his own age with a slight build and bright blonde hair. As Stewart looked at the man's back a feeling of unease arose inside him. It manifested first as a stab of discomfort in his stomach, then as a dull ache in his abdomen. With some surprise he recognised it as fear.

The other customer turned his head slightly to look along the shelves, revealing his profile. Stewart took in a sharp breath, almost a gasp, as he recognised the face. There was now a reason for his sudden anxiety. He was looking at an old enemy, and although he had not at first seen the face, he had subconsciously reacted to something about the head and stance. A long-buried dread had been triggered and caused his insides to lurch. It was Lenny Sparks, or Sparkie, leader of the bully pack at school.

In those far-off days it had been an honour to belong to Sparkie's gang. By sheer force of the devilment of his personality, Lenny Sparks had attracted to himself all the worst behaved boys, who thought nothing of surrounding a pupil and stealing his dinner money – and anything else worth having – and then subjecting him to whatever physical violence there was time for.

Lenny had terrorised Stewart – then a pale quiet child – for years. An easy target for bullies, Stewart had been obliged to work out strategies for not being caught on the way to school, robbed and going hungry for the rest of the day. He would lie in bed at night dreaming of how he would stand up to Sparkie one day, fantasising his way to becoming a hero to all the victims, yet waking up the next morning to a churning stomach and sweaty palms, despising himself.

"Your usual, sir?" asked the shop assistant.

"Not tonight. I'll have a bottle of champagne. Cheap one will do. I've gotta girl to impress. Know what I mean?"

"Oh yes, sir. How about this one?"

"Just the job. Got some fancy wrapping?"

Stewart listened to the voice of the man, but there was something in the resonance which made him clearly remember the voice of the boy. He looked with curiosity at his old adversary, noting how small and insignificant his appearance was in contrast to his own. He remembered overhearing one of the teachers describing Lenny as 'a street urchin of the worst type' and wondering whether any of them knew about the gang's reign of terror.

"Thank you, sir," said the assistant as he took Lenny's money and handed him a plastic bag containing a gaudily wrapped bottle of champagne. Stewart stood aside to let Lenny pass, recoiling involuntarily as the small man brushed against him.

"And now what can I do for you, sir?" the assistant asked Stewart, who was looking at Lenny's retreating back.

"Nothing – I've changed my mind," said Stewart with an apologetic smile as he hurried out of the shop. On the pavement he looked about him and then saw Lenny disappearing around a corner. Stewart hurried to the corner, almost running, then saw his prey walking past a row of shops. Taking long strides, Stewart caught up with Lenny just as he was slipping into an alley with two bollards at its entrance. He allowed the other to reach the middle of the alley before stepping in front of him and obliging him to stop.

"Tables are turned now, Sparkie," said Stewart quietly. He looked down into the long-forgotten face, older than its years through street-wise experience from the age of six, etched with quick-witted opportunism and the casual cruelty of the habitual bully.

"What? Who are you then?" Lenny's eyes were wide with anxiety. "What do you want?"

Stewart smiled sweetly. "I want that bag you're holding."

"Why?"

"No good reason. Just because it's yours, Sparkie. Just because I want something for nothing, something that belongs to somebody else. Just because I'm in a position of power over you, Sparkie. Just because I can. You of all people will understand that."

Lenny glanced around, but there was nobody near to help him escape from this large and inexplicably threatening stranger.

"It's no use looking for help, Sparkie. There's no gang of nasty little bullies like yourself to back you up. You're nobody's hero now, you're on your own. Horrible isn't it? A bad feeling, isn't it? I know all about that bad feeling, Sparkie. I could almost be sorry for you. But you know what? I'm not."

"Who the hell *are* you?" Lenny was sweating, his face white and his eyes staring.

Stewart reached out and pushed him back against the wall. "What did you do with all that dinner money, Sparkie?"

"Eh?"

"The money you and your weasly little thugs stole from kids like me at school. Did you buy sweets? Booze? Drugs?"

Lenny suddenly understood and gave a sickly grin. "Oh, I get it. Long time ago, eh? What's your name? Can't say I recognise you."

"Stewart. Stewart Black. Remember?"

"Oh yeah! Stewpot – little squinty Stewpot. Wouldn't say boo to a goose." Lenny tried to step aside but two huge hands slapped against the wall, one on each side of his head.

"Not so little now, am I?"

"S'pose not," said Lenny warily. "Here, you mustn't take all that seriously, you know. As I said – long time ago."

"Mustn't take it seriously? *Mustn't take it seriously?*" A large hand came around and grabbed a handful of Lenny's newly-laundered shirt, his 'impress-a-girl' shirt. "Have you the remotest idea of what you were doing to other kids' lives?"

Lenny shook his head, eyeing Stewart with suspicion. "Look, Stewart, we were only kids. Kids do these things. What's the big deal?"

"The big deal is this. Every time I saw you coming, my stomach turned over and my knees felt weak. Just the sight of you made me feel sick. How dare you do that to me or anybody else! What right had you to load our lives with so much downright misery? The mugging and the violence happened on the way to school, then in the school playground, then again on the way home. Only at weekends were we safe from your disgusting greedy cruelty. It wasn't until I left and went to another school that I began to put on weight and grow taller." Stewart tightened his grip on the shirt. "Look at me now, Sparkie. Not such a squinty-eyed little git now, am I?"

Lenny eyed the broad shoulders and muscular neck, then looked around wildly for help.

"Look at me, Lenny. Note the difference now. I work out at the gym. I swim. I row. Most useful of all... I box and wrestle."

Lenny was now panting with terror. "Here – what's your game then?" he gasped.

"No game, Sparkie. Oh dearie me, where are your gang, your minders? All alone, are you? That's bad, isn't it? Here's little Stewart all grown up and big, and there's little Lenny Sparks all grown up and small. Funny old world, isn't it?"

"Get out of my way or I'll..."

"Yes? You'll what? Come on then, Sparkie the tough guy, Sparkie the thief. What are you going to do now? I'll tell you. You're going to give me that bag. And if you don't I'm going to punch your lights out and *then* take the bag. Understand, bully boy?"

"There's only a bottle in this bag, nothing else."

"Oh good – I know a little lady who'll appreciate that."

By now Lenny was shaking all over. "It was only fun! We didn't mean any harm..."

"Fun! To you that living nightmare was fun? You poisoned my whole life. Do you realise that some kids commit suicide because of scum like you?" Stewart tightened his grip. "How do you feel now, Sparkie? What are you going to do now, leader of the pack? Want my dinner money, do you? I'll tell you what I want – I want that bag."

"Take it then, damn you! But take your hand off me!"

Stewart smiled contentedly and released the little man. "That's better, Sparkie," he said, reaching for the bag. "This has been your come-uppance – fear and loss, the same things you inflicted on others. Not nice, is it? Fear of being hurt by a bully and losing your champagne. Now I want to see you run away along this alley as fast as your cowardly little legs can carry you. Off you go then!"

***

Jane was just finishing off both the crab salad starters when the bell rang. When she opened the door, Stewart stood there smiling and holding a plastic bag. She stood aside to let him in, unsmiling. He bent to give her a kiss.

"You smell like fish or something," he remarked as she closed the door. A girl who had taken care to smell right with English Rose body spray could scarcely be pleased.

"That's the crab starter. I've just eaten both of them."

"You've eaten my starter?" He glanced at his watch. "Oh lord – look, I'm really sorry. Fact is, I've just had a marvellous adventure. If you'll let me open this champagne while you fetch suitable glasses I'll tell you all about it. What's the main course?"

"Fish pie."

"We seem to be having rather a fishy evening, don't we? What's for pud – baked shrimps and custard?"

Jane declined to answer. They sat at the table and when Stewart had opened the bottle he filled the glasses, then sat and watched the bubbles.

"Well? Aren't we going to drink it then?"

"In a second. I'm just savouring the moment."

Jane squinted at the label. "Why? It's a quite unremarkable champagne. I've got a nice Cotes du Rhone in the kitchen."

"It's more than just champagne. It's fate. It's Kismet. It's karma. It's what goes around comes around. It's come-uppance. That bottle is full of school dinners."

"Now you've lost me. School dinners?"

"Now listen, I've a story to tell. There was once a small boy called Stewart Black…"

The Rainbow Came And Went

After Edna Brown had fallen from a swing onto her head at the age of two, she could no longer see colours. Her perception of the world around her was in black, white and grey – as though she existed in an old movie. From being a sensitive and active toddler, curious about everything from a ladybird on a leaf to a passing helicopter, she became passive and stolid, unimaginative to a degree.

In compensation she became obsessively interested in shapes and numbers, which eventually resulted in her becoming a teacher of geometry and mathematics. Her unawareness of colours led to her bizarre dress sense and gave her pupils plenty of amusement. On entering a classroom she was usually greeted with delighted grins which she took to mean that they were pleased to see her, not hearing such muttered comments as 'here come the walking paintbox' or 'sunglasses at the ready'.

In her dreams she remembered colours, but in her waking life she thought little about it except for the inconvenience of being unable to drive a car. "I don't really mind about not driving," she told a friend. "It looks dangerous to me. I'm all for a quiet life."

The quiet life lasted until she was thirty-five, when at last she felt ready for adventure. She booked herself in for a cruise to Norway with many misgivings, wondering what she was letting herself in for. On the day of her embarkation her married friends June and Derek drove her to the London dock and accompanied her as far as they could.

"Time to get aboard now, I think," said Edna. "June, thank you so much for helping me choose the right clothes. I can see I shall have to come to you in future for advice."

"Any time. You look so nice with the right clothes and make-up. Now don't go mixing them all up, will you?"

"Not a chance," grinned Edna. "Everything's labelled."

"We'll be here to pick you up when you get back," promised Derek.

Edna entered life on board in her usual state of detached acceptance. One particular pleasure was to find a quiet place on a lower deck and look down at the dark foaming water appearing to rush past the boat. She would look down at it until she felt that she too was being sped away with the water. A daily irritation, for her and for many other passengers, was being unable to use the seats placed specially beside extra wide windows, for the purpose of viewing the passing scenery. These seats were daily occupied by members of a pensioners' group for the sole purpose of morning and after-lunch sleeping, mouths open and snoring whilst spectacular views slipped past unappreciated.

One night, as they were nearing the Norwegian coast, it was Edna's turn to be invited to sit at the Captain's table with a group of others. She accepted the invitation phlegmatically and rummaged through her clothes, picking out colours according to careful labels. Satisfied with her choice, she made her way to the appropriate dining room where the Captain stood ready to shake hands with his guests. When it came to her turn the world turned upside down. One glance at the Captain and she was lost.

The Captain was lean-featured with a deep tan. His eyes were sea-grey and his hair was black. Edna was unaware of his tan but she was able to register the grey eyes and dark hair. There was something about the features which captivated her with astonishing speed. As he took her hand in his, she experienced a feverish thrill which was almost like falling into a pyrexial illness. When it became apparent that she was to sit next to him she could scarcely breathe. She could only toy with her food whilst he asked polite questions. Whenever he turned to speak to the passenger on his other side, Edna felt bereft. She wished that the evening would never end.

As she looked down at her plate, she was puzzled to see some florets of broccoli pulsating very slightly. Then, slowly at first, the broccoli turned green. Dark green. Then suddenly the whole plate was full of colour – the bright orange of carrots, the creamy whiteness of little new potatoes, the yellow of the sweetcorn, the green of the broccoli.

Edna looked up from her plate and gasped as she saw a kaleidoscope of colour in the room. The Captain was talking to a passenger in a mauve dress with a filmy pink scarf flung around her shoulders. The carpeted floor was patterned red. The table flowers were golden marigolds in a blue bowl with some tastefully arranged pale green leaves. There were pictures in vivid colours all around the walls. It was like living one of her night-time dreams.

She looked up as the Captain turned back to her. "And is this your first sea voyage, Miss Brown?"

"Oh yes," she said breathlessly. "But do call me Edna."

"Right. Edna. And have you got your sealegs yet?"

"Yes, no problem." She looked at him and saw the colour of his tanned skin. She felt dizzy with the effects of his nearness and the dazzling impact of the surrounding colours. It was more than her nervous system could cope with, and she slumped sideways in a dead faint.

When she opened her eyes she was lying on a couch in the sick bay. Her first impression was of colours everywhere. Directly in front of her she saw a print of Van Gogh's 'Sunflowers' hanging against a pale blue wall.

"Feeling better now, Miss Brown?" The female nurse was smiling down at her encouragingly.

Edna looked up and marvelled at the golden curls escaping from beneath the white cap, the clear blue eyes and the delicate pink-and-white complexion.

"Yes, thank you. Did I faint? I don't remember."

"It was probably all the excitement of your first voyage. Are you enjoying it?" The nurse took Edna's wrist and felt for her pulse.

"Oh yes – wonderful! How did you know it was my first voyage?"

"My husband told me."

"Your husband? I don't think I know him, do I?"

"Yes, you do. You were sitting next to him at dinner. He's the Captain."

It was as though a bucket of ice water had drenched her. "Oh yes, the Captain," she murmured, closing her eyes. "I remember telling him." A coldness had settled inside her.

"You're looking a good deal better than when you came in here," smiled the nurse.

"Am I? Can I see? Is there a hand mirror somewhere?"

"Borrow mine." The nurse went to a side table and took a small mirror from a drawer.

Edna looked at her reflection without enthusiasm. She saw a square-jawed face, straight eyebrows, a long thin nose and an uncompromising mouth, all framed by limp brown hair. A geometrical face, she thought. Scarcely female at all. Not like this pretty young thing with the yellow curls.

"My husband will be along to see you soon. He was quite concerned about you."

As the girl said these words, Edna saw a change in her reflection. A slight pink had stained her cheeks and there was a softening around the mouth at the idea of the Captain wanting to see her.

"Thanks," she said, handing back the mirror and hoping the girl had not seen her reaction. "I think I would like to go to my cabin now. Please tell the Captain there is no need for him to see me, but that I am grateful for his concern."

"Alright, but sit up first and see how you feel. Don't want any more fainting, do we?"

The next morning Edna stood looking through her cabin window at breathtaking scenery. Glittering sea, blue sky, the rugged coastline with its waterfalls tumbling from mountain fissures and cascading over rocks towards the sea. Her change of vision had been maintained.

She went up on deck to get a wider view. It was still early and there were not many people about. Everything seemed to have a still and dream-like quality. The flow of air against her cheeks was a magical tingle, seeming to touch something in her memory connecting her with early childhood. She drew in a deep breath, as though trying to inhale the very essence of Norway itself.

"Good morning, Edna!"

She held onto the ship's safety rail, her knees weakening, before turning to face the Captain, who was coming towards her with his arm around the pretty nurse of the night before.

"So glad to see you've recovered. You gave us all a fright."

"Yes, sorry about that. How did I get to the sick bay?"

"Easy. I picked you up and carried you," grinned the Captain.

Edna trembled at the thought of his arms supporting her. "Well, thank you for helping me. I don't know what came over me. I'm not usually given to attacks of the vapours. Your wife was so kind to me."

"This is my last tour," said the girl. "We're pregnant, aren't we darling?"

I don't want to know! Edna screamed silently. "Oh, congratulations! Do you want a boy or a girl?"

The girl shrugged. "Don't mind as long as it's healthy and has all the right bits and pieces."

"Well, I'm off to an early breakfast," said Edna briskly. "I need stoking up after not eating last night. See you around!"

The tawny brown of the coffee, the gold of the marmalade, the yellow of the scrambled eggs, the multi-hued flowers in the vase – Edna devoured the colours hungrily as she ate the food. She was trying to come to terms with being flung into two different dimensions at once – attraction towards a man for the first time, plus seeing all the colours of her dreams in daylight. She realised that the first had triggered the second, that something physiological had taken place in her damaged nervous system and effected a connection which allowed normal functioning.

On the voyage back from the Arctic Circle, Edna's time was spent trying to spot the Captain. She would never have tried to come too close, only to look and drink in his appearance, trying to etch his features on her memory for the future she knew she would be facing alone. All the while the surrounding colours – the scenery, the ship's décor, the clothes of the other passengers – seemed to sing out in a kind of celestial radiance. The Captain would have been astounded if he had known what miracle he had unleashed in the person of the quiet and colourless Edna Brown.

One day, as the ship was heading for home waters and rolling in a sudden squall, Edna was making for the safety of her cabin when in a dim corner of the corridor she spotted the Captain. To her horror he was locked in an unmistakeable amorous clinch with the girl singer of the ship's band. For one frozen moment she stared, then she turned and fled before they could see her.

"What are you crying for, you fool?" she asked her reflection in her cabin mirror. "He's betrayed his wife, not you. He scarcely knows you exist. You are just another dowdy single female passenger he's paid to be charming to."

She didn't go to the dining hall that night but concentrated on her packing, throwing her clothes untidily into her suitcase and ignoring the carefully devised labelling system. Then she went to bed early with a Mars bar and a paperback novel, not even bothering to use moisturiser on her face and hands.

When she awoke the next morning she was aware of the absence of all colour as soon as she opened her eyes. She lay looking around at the familiar monochrome tones and thought, *Edna's herself again. Good. Better that way.*

June and Derek were on the quay to meet her when the ship docked. "Had a good time, darling?" asked June as they hugged.

Thank heaven for friends, thought Edna. "Yes thanks, lovely. Do you know, when we were in the Arctic Circle people were actually sunbathing on deck, would you believe? Bare feet, shorts, suntops, the lot!"

"And how did you get on with clothes? I hope you've packed them carefully so that you can use them again."

"Didn't bother. After all," she glanced quickly at the docked ship, "it's over."

Later she climbed into the back seat of the car as Derek locked her luggage into the boot. All the way home, as June plied her with questions, a separate voice in her head was repeating, *It's over... it's over... it's over...*

Mirror Of Transformations

"Matty, my dear," said Mr Paget with as much patience as he could muster, "I really do think it is time your sister went to stay with your Cousin Rose again. We have had her for a good three months, and you know the arrangement was that each household would take her for no longer than six weeks at a time. I don't wish to be difficult, but..."

"Yes, Henry, I know. But... I do so dread having to tell her. You know how attached to me she is."

"All the same, three months is not six weeks, is it?"

Matilda's stomach churned and a worried frown creased her pale forehead. "It was so unfortunate that she had that accident just before she was due to depart for Rose's home. I am afraid she has become habituated to being here with us."

Henry pursed his lips. "If only she had not stepped into the road to give a coin to that wretched little crossing-sweeper, none of this would have happened. The coach driver had no chance to pull the horses over in time. I witnessed the whole thing from my study window. Now here she is firmly entrenched without any remembrance that we share her visits with Rose and your brother Edward – neither of whom have come to see her during her convalescence, I venture to add."

Matilda flushed guiltily, feeling her family's remiss behaviour to reflect on herself. "I'll speak to her today," she murmured, picking up the teapot. "And I'll write to Rose. More tea, Henry?"

"No thank you, my dear," said Henry, looking at the watch he had drawn from his waistcoat pocket. "I must be at the office soon. I am to interview a new clerk today and I am already a little late. I shall have to hail a cab."

Matilda accompanied her husband to the front door and helped him on with his greatcoat. She watched him as he hurried down the front steps and hailed a cab drawn by a tired-looking chestnut mare. Just before he climbed aboard he turned and called to his wife, "Today, Matty! Speak to Patience and write to Rose."

Matilda nodded, waved, and then turned back into the house with a sigh. She closed the front door firmly and made her way reluctantly towards the stairs, where the maid was on her way down carrying a tray.

"Jenny, has Miss Patience made a good breakfast this morning? Yesterday she ate so little."

"Oh yes, ma'am. Look at the tray – not a scrap left. She's got 'er appetite back an' no mistake."

"Thank you, Jenny. I'll go up and see her now. Oh, by the way – who is she today?"

"Elizabeth Bennett, she says, ma'am."

"Hm. Yesterday she was Nell Gwyn."

"Yes ma'am."

***

Patience Woods was sitting up in bed awaiting her morning visit from her sister Matty. She was as dark as her sister was fair, but with slightly coarser features. A not unpleasant face, but without Matilda's refinement. The face of a pretty peasant, Henry had once remarked.

The door opened and Matilda came into the room, smiling resolutely.

"Good morning, Patty. I hope you slept well?"

The woman in the bed turned to face Matilda, her expression one of welcome as she held out her hand. "Ah, Jane! Come and sit beside me. Tell me your news. When are you to see Mr Bingley again?"

Matilda sat in the chair beside the bed and took the proffered hand. "Now Patty, please try to be yourself. You know you can if you try. Just concentrate. I am not Jane Bennett, I am your sister Matty. Matty and Patty, remember?"

Patience's eyes suddenly had a hunted look. "I do not know what you mean, Jane. I await a visit from Mr Darcy. Perhaps Mr Bingley will come too, do you think? Oh Jane, would it not be perfect if we were to have a double wedding?"

Matilda withdrew her hand and gazed sadly at her sister. The delusions had begun when Patience had been jilted a week before her wedding to a wealthy businessman, who had become enamoured of a younger and prettier – not to say richer – woman. A breach-of-promise case had ensued and Patience had been awarded a considerable sum of money after prolonged wrangling, but by then

Patience had descended into a breakdown and the delusions had started to happen. In these delusions Patience always played the role of a woman adored by an altogether desirable man, and Matilda could plainly see that her sister's damaged mind was always in denial of her rejection, continually trying to salve her deep emotional wound by pretending that someone loved her.

In a rare moment of irritation, Matilda blurted out, "What happened to Nell Gwyn? Did you tire of her?"

Patience turned her head and looked towards the window to where an ancient apple tree tapped unpruned twigs against the pane. "Ah yes," she whispered. "Let not poor Nellie starve. How that man loved me. He would love me still if he was able."

"Patty dear, look at me."

Patience withdrew her gaze from the window and looked anxiously at her sister. She seemed like a cornered animal, reluctant to expose her vulnerability.

"Patty, you are my dear little sister Patience. We grew up together and you know quite well who I am. You have been ill for a while, but you will recover. You will come back to yourself. You are not Elizabeth Bennett and I am not Jane. You are not Nell Gwyn or anybody else but yourself. Where do all these people come from, Patty – and why?"

Patience glanced at a hand mirror resting on the beside table. "I see them," she murmured. "I become them. They are me. I am them."

Matilda followed her gaze. She reached out and picked up the mirror.

"Oh don't!" cried Patience in sudden alarm. "You must not… it is not for you! You should not look in that mirror!"

"Why not?"

"Give it to me. It is for my eyes alone. The gypsy told me."

"Do you mean that gypsy at the fair when we were girls? The one who gave you the mirror when she told your fortune?"

"Yes, but she did not tell my fortune. She simply gave me the mirror and said that it would one day save me. She said I would remember it in the hour of my greatest need. I tried to give her money for it, but she refused."

"And then you told me you had lost it."

"No, I did not lose it. I wrapped it up and hid it. I forgot about it until after Gerald – found a more attractive partner. Then I remembered what the gypsy said and I retrieved the mirror. Matty, I should have gone quite mad without it. Believe me, I am not mad. I am quietly conducting myself back to a normal frame of mind, *but in my own way*. Do you see?"

"Patty, you are now speaking to me more rationally than you have for months. Does that mean you no longer feel that you are Elizabeth Bennett?"

"Oh no, Matty. I am Elizabeth Bennett and shall remain so for all of this day. It is my salvation, you see. It protects me. Bear with it, Matty. It is leading me back to sanity. Tomorrow I shall look in the mirror and it will show me who I am to be for that day. Now give me the mirror, but on no account look into it yourself."

Matilda knew she had to humour her sister. She rose, placed the mirror face downwards on the table and went to the window. Keeping her back to her sister she said, "Today I must write to Cousin Rose. You are now quite recovered from your accident and we must resume the original arrangement. You have been with us for three months now, Patty. I am sure you understand that it would be best if we return to our usual six-week arrangement with Rose, Edward and ourselves."

There was a silence, then Patience said, "This is Henry speaking, of course."

Matilda turned from the window. "Henry was extremely good when you had your accident. It was he who saw that you would have to stay here until you were fit to go to Rose. I was grateful when he suggested it when the doctor was all for sending you to the hospital."

"Give me another month here with you, Matty." Patience's eyes were dark with anxiety. "One more month. That will suffice, I know it will."

Matilda moved towards the door. "I shall leave you to get dressed now, Patty. We shall take a few extra turns around the garden this morning. Your legs grow stronger every day now."

As Matilda passed through the doorway, Patience called to her. "And if that odious Mr Collins calls again, tell Papa to tell him I would not marry him if he were the last man in the world!"

Matilda left the room without another word.

***

At six o'clock Matilda was in the hallway helping Henry off with his coat.

"Well, Matty? How did matters go with you and Patience? Did you speak to her? Did you send that letter to Rose?"

"I wrote the letter," said Matilda as they went into the drawing-room, "but I have not yet sent it."

"No matter, Jenny can post it in the morning. But did you speak to Patience?"

"Yes."

"Good. And...?"

Matilda twisted her handkerchief between agitated fingers. "Oh Henry – she is not sufficiently recovered."

Henry made an impatient gesture. "But she is now so much improved that she walks all around the garden as far as the brook and back! Why bother to write the letter when you have already decided she is still unfit?"

"She is unwell still in her mind, Henry. Physically she is much improved, but mentally she is in a strange halfway state. Today we had an almost normal conversation, then she reverted to being someone else. I discovered where these different illusions are coming from."

"Oh?"

"Yes. She believes it is because of an old mirror given to her years ago by a gypsy."

"What are you saying, Matty?" said Henry, staring at his wife as if she too were out of her mind.

"It was years ago, We were only young girls. The gypsy told her that one day the mirror would save her in her time of need."

"Save her? From what?"

"She kept the mirror hidden for years – waiting for some dreadful event to come along, I suppose. Then after Gerald jilted her and she had the breakdown, she thought the time had come to see if the gypsy's mirror could help her. She unwrapped it after all these years and looked into it."

"And I suppose she imagined it had miraculous powers?" scoffed Henry. "Really, Matty..."

"Henry, please let me continue. This is where all these different characters are coming from. Patience claims that the mirror tells her who to become every morning. Today she is Elizabeth Bennett."

Henry stared. "And how, pray, is that supposed to lead her back to sanity?" He jumped to his feet. "This is preposterous! This must stop!" He began top pace back and forth, hands behind his back and scowling. "She will drive herself completely insane."

"On the contrary, Henry. It appears to be helping her back to normality. Today we held a lucid conversation for quite a few minutes."

Henry stopped pacing. "Where is she now?"

"Sitting in the garden, enjoying the last of the evening sun."

"Good! I shall go up to her room and smash that damned mirror. This unhealthiness must stop."

"No, Henry! You may be doing irreparable harm! I tell you she is improving in both body and mind and may soon be well enough to go to Rose."

Henry was past listening to the voice of reason. He hurried from the room and took the stairs two at a time, while Matilda hurried into the garden and sat beside her sister, holding her hand very tightly.

***

"What?" screamed Patience. "He is going to smash my mirror? But he will smash my mind! Does he not know that? I stand on the brink of recovery, and he would push me back into the abyss. Go and stop him!"

There came the sound of a startled oath, then the unmistakeable splintering of glass. Matilda knew from the sound that Henry had smashed the mirror against the marble washstand which stood by the window.

The two women jumped to their feet and stared up at the bedroom window. Patience gave a hoarse cry, and then crumpled senseless to the ground.

As she knelt and tried to revive her sister, Matilda heard the sound of footsteps on the flagstones. She looked up and saw Henry coming towards her. She noticed that one of his hands was bleeding slightly. She got to her feet, pulled a handkerchief from her pocket and reached for his hand.

"A mere scratch, lady," said Henry in a strange voice. "The fortunes of war."

"What?" Something in his demeanour had turned her cold.

"I must go now."

"Go? Go where?"

Jenny appeared from around the corner of the house. "Dinner is ready now, ma'am," she said, and went back into the house.

"What do you mean, Henry?"

"There is much yet to be done. Provisions to arrange, men to arm, animals to muster…"

"What animals?" Matilda's heart was pounding.

"The elephants, Brave, strong creatures…"

"What elephants?" She was now shaking all over, remembering the oath she had heard before the glass had shattered.

"The creatures who will carry men, arms, water and provision over the mountain passes."

Matilda put her hand to her head and swayed.

"Who are you?" she whispered in dread.

"You ask me – ME – who I am when the whole world knows me?" He raised his head proudly. "I am Hannibal."

Aghast, Matilda reached up and touched his face. "Henry, listen to me. Did you look in the mirror before you smashed it?"

But Henry seemed not to hear. His eyes were scanning distant horizons, his ears were hearing far-off sounds.

"Are you coming in, ma'am?" called Jenny. "Soup's on the table."

Matilda looked helplessly from the rapt expression on her husband's face to the inert figure of her sister and thought – *what now?*